T0355062

FILTHY DIRTY LOVE

STACEY KENNEDY

This book is a work of fiction. Names, characters, places, and incidents are the product of the author's imagination or are used fictitiously. Any resemblance to actual events, locales, or persons, living or dead, is coincidental.

Stacey Kennedy
www.staceykennedy.com

Edited by Christa Soule
Copy Edited by Chelle Olson, Literally Addicted to Detail
Cover Design and Cover Photograph by Sara Eirew

Manufactured in Canada
First Edition January 2017

As always, for my readers.

Prologue

Bedroom eyes had been watching her most of the night, and Joss couldn't take it anymore. She'd eye fucked him on the dance floor until he finally joined her, and she'd spent the last half an hour grinding into him in what he obviously read as an invitation.

The minute the stylish single bathroom door clicked shut and locked, sex packaged in a black T-shirt and dark blue jeans was on her. He strode forward, sending her walking backward until her back slammed against the bathroom wall in Seattle's hottest dance club, Wicked. His tongue dove into her mouth, overwhelming her, while his lips rhythmically danced with hers. His hands explored her back and her bottom, squeezing her cheeks tightly.

"Damn, sugar, you taste good," he murmured, dropping his head onto her shoulder and nuzzling her neck.

Her eyes rolled into the back of her head as his breath fluttered across her flesh just below her ear. If her panties weren't already drenched from the confidence in his low, sultry voice, the feeling of strength in his hard body against hers sealed the deal. She thrust her hands into his stylish, gelled, light brown hair, begging him to lift his head. She needed that mouth on hers.

When he finally did look at her, butterflies fluttered within her belly. This guy didn't draw desire out of her; he yanked it out of her soul. His hand came to her chin while he stared at her.

No, while he *examined* her, in the same way she couldn't stop looking at him. Broad shoulders. Ripped arms. Chiseled jaw. Short beard. Intense blue eyes that had the special little something that made her decide he would be her first one-night stand. Something powerful and potent. Something real and intense.

Then, still staring deeply into her eyes, he broke the silence. "I feel like I'm biting into the forbidden fruit with you."

"The forbidden fruit?" she repeated, breathless.

He watched her, brows drawn tight. "You don't seem like the type of girl who has a quickie in the bathroom of a bar."

"What makes you say that?" she asked.

His mouth twitched as he dragged a thumb across her bottom lip. "You seem like a very good girl, who plays very much by the rules."

"I'm the one who instigated this, so I'm not sure why you think that." She didn't want to be a *good girl.* Tonight, she wanted to be as bad as she could possibly be.

"No, sweetheart." He gave her an arrogant smile. "I instigated this. You simply reacted to my offer." He tucked her hair behind her ear, then watched his fingers trace her jawline. "I want to make sure you understand this is a one-time deal. I'm not looking for a girlfriend. I won't call you after tonight. You'll never see me again. Are you sure you won't wake up tomorrow with a world of regret?"

She startled a little at his honesty. Her ex-boyfriend Nick, who'd ended their six-year relationship over the phone, didn't have an honest bone in his sleazeball body. Nor did he care what she thought about anything. His feelings always came first.

Odd, she thought. Weren't one-night stands supposed to be all about regretting them the next day? She smiled at bedroom eyes and leaned into his hand. "I don't regret this now. I won't regret it tomorrow." In the morning, she left for the police academy. Finding a boyfriend was the last thing on her mind. Tonight was all about forgetting Nick, ignoring that he'd thought her life in Seattle was too boring. About disregarding the heartbreak. This moment was all about taking something that she wanted because she could. "I want this. I want you."

"That's good enough for me." The thickness of his body pushed her thighs apart and his erection pressed against the junction between her legs. She rocked against him, and he grinned. "You like that, do you?" He shoved her skirt over her hips, and grabbed her legs, allowing them to wrap around his hips as he pinned her to the wall.

"God, yes." She held onto his shoulders and ground herself against him again, unable to help it. That's what this guy did to her. He made her reach for pleasure, to not be shy about what she craved.

Unable to get enough of him, wanting desperately to be closer and far more naked, she shifted her hips, rubbing her panty-covered clit against the front of his jeans, feeling the thickness of his cock. He dropped his head against her neck, and the scruff on his cheeks brushed across her skin. She shivered as he licked and nibbled and swirled his tongue until her breathing deepened and her body flushed with unnatural heat. Only then did he take her lips again, kissing her in a way she'd only fantasized about.

Dominant. Possessive.

Each time his tongue dove into her mouth, he owned her fully and completely. And *fuck,* the guy could kiss. There was nothing messy and unsure about the way he moved. His sculpted lips were amazing. His tongue sensually stroking hers was perfection. He tasted like *man.*

Using his shoulders to gain leverage, she rocked her hips, her breath speeding up, her heart pounding. He growled against her mouth, and she shivered, losing herself in the power he exuded. His growl came again, this time throatier. She shifted faster and harder against him, digging her nails into his shoulders.

Then his piercing eyes met hers, studying her intently. A slow smile spread across his face. "Oh, sugar, I like you."

His voice. Good Lord, that voice had power, one that surely shouldn't belong to anyone. It made her needy and desperate. She prided herself on her control, but when it came to this guy, she had none. It didn't matter that she was in a bathroom at a bar. It didn't matter that she'd only just met him. She wanted him to ravage her in a very dirty and filthy way.

Eyes on her, he licked his lips, and his brows drew together. Intense. Passionate. Determined. He grabbed her butt cheeks and began shifting her against his cock, bringing her to the edge. The way he watched her with those captivating eyes sent her soaring.

"Yes, girl, give me what I want," he stated.

And just like that, she did.

She wrapped her arms around his neck and trembled against him. Her moans cut off, and her breath became stuck in her throat. All she could do was hang onto him while she rode out her quivering orgasm.

Then she crashed…and crashed *hard,* panting and whimpering.

Only when the world realigned, and she felt the wetness of his lips brushing against hers, pulling her slowly back from the high, could she even think about moving. She forced her eyes open, finding his gaze locked on hers, his sinful smile instantly warming her.

"Christ, you are a sexy little thing," he told her, releasing her wobbly legs.

He yanked the front of her top down until her breast was exposed and the tight nipple stood out, begging for his mouth. His low moan of obvious delight tightened her thighs as he grasped her breast in his strong hand. He dragged his mouth across her nipple and groaned. "I could play with this perfect body all night long," he told her, sucking her taut bud to the roof of his mouth.

Being already oversensitive, she gasped, unable to stand still as his mouth popped off, only to suck deeper the next time. She grasped his thick forearms, loving how the muscles flexed beneath her touch as he yanked down the other side of her shirt and bra, exposing her other nipple to the cool air. When he sucked deeply, a loud knock on the door echoed against the bathroom walls.

"Ignore it," he said.

She decided she didn't care about the damn door, as he released her breast and began sliding his palm slowly up her thigh. Her breathing deepened when he nudged her skirt up, his hand coming closer and closer to where she wanted him.

Another knock banged against the door, shaking it on its hinges, yet his hand moved higher…and higher still. He tucked his fingers into the side of her panties, sliding over her slick heat.

The side of his mouth arched. "Soaking wet, sugar?" he murmured. "Do you always get so hot so easily?"

She leaned her head back against the wall and squeezed her eyes shut, "No."

"Ah, so you like me touching you?" he asked softly, stroking her swollen clit with light flicks of his finger.

"Yes," she whispered, not even understanding how he made her this aroused. The man had gifts. Magical ones.

His finger froze. "Look at me."

She reopened her eyes and found the look of a man who knew his worth.

"Only me?" he repeated.

Something so powerful crossed between them, it was at once frightening and exhilarating. Something she'd never experienced before with Nick. He'd always made love for his orgasm, not hers. This passion was addictive. A night she'd surely never forget.

"Only you," she answered honestly.

"That's a sexy answer coming from a very pretty mouth." He slid his thumb gently over her throbbing clit, back and forth, teasing the little bud. "You have a choice to make. You can leave this bathroom now and take what I've already given you. Or you can let me give you all that I have to give."

Instead of using dirty words she was never very good at and usually ended up blushing over, she reached for his belt. She unhooked the leather and then shoved his pants and boxer briefs down, watching his mouth curve. His thick cock sprang free, and she began stroking him. When she dragged her hand over the thick, bulging veins straining for release and up to the rounded tip, he gave a guttural moan.

Determined to pleasure him in the way he had her, she slid her finger over the slit, gathering his pre-cum and sliding the silkiness over his cock head. He reached for the front of his T-shirt, pulling it over his head to rest on the back of his neck, giving her a fine view of his ripped body. From a squared chest to a well-defined six-pack to a V at the waist, he clearly spent a lot of time in the gym. Not too big to look ridiculous but not too thin either.

Gloriously perfect.

She bit her bottom lip and traced the valleys of his muscles, feeling each one flex beneath her finger. Slowly, and not caring who knocked on the door, she let herself explore the body she couldn't even believe she got to touch. The guys she'd met in university didn't look like this.

This guy was all man. All delicious, fuckable man.

"You're…" She gazed into his powerful eyes and lost her voice.

His left eyebrow rose. "I'm *what*?"

She felt drunk from the endorphins as she glanced at his body once more before meeting his gaze again. "You're so damn hot."

His grin was full of sin. "Tell me what you want, sugar."

"I want you." She grabbed his thick cock and used his pre-cum again to lubricate him as she stroked, urging him to take her.

"Inside you?" His hips shot forward, and he thrust himself into her hand.

"Yes. Fuck me."

His eyes flared. Obviously, he appreciated boldness. He reached for his pants at his knees, taking out his wallet and then grabbing a condom.

When she moved her touch away, he tsked. "I was enjoying those hands."

Heat flushed through her, and she began stroking him again. His low moan slid sensually over her, flooding her with urgency. He watched her as she slowly dragged her hand over his shaft from base to tip, memorizing the feel of his dick. She took his heavy balls into her hand before teasing them with light touches. He groaned, and his jaw clenched as he unwrapped the condom.

That left eyebrow arched again. "Since you're so good with your hands…" He offered the condom.

Desperation consumed her as she took the condom and quickly applied the latex over his shaft. She only looked away for a moment before she stared into those intense eyes again, letting him see how much she liked touching him. Allowing him to witness how crazy he made her.

As soon as she'd fully sheathed him, his hands were on her face, his mouth on hers again, slowly nipping her until he deepened the kiss, taking her to a place that inflamed her body. God, she could feel everything. Every whisper of breath from his nose. Every slide of his thumbs across her cheeks. *He* became all she knew as his condom-covered cock rested against her stomach.

"I won't be gentle," he murmured across her mouth.

"Good," was all she got out before he spun her around.

The cool metal of the bathroom stall pressed against her taut nipples, her cheek resting there, too. She stared into the heat of his eyes in the mirror next to them above the sink.

He slid his hand up to her neck, holding tightly. "Do you see how sexy you are? How much I want you?"

"Yes." Her voice cracked with urgency. Her legs began shaking, but it wasn't nervousness. It was pure, unadulterated desire.

Intensity washed over his expression when he removed her panties and then grabbed her ass, spreading her cheeks. She felt the tip of his cock press against her, and then with a shift of his hips, he thrust deeply inside.

She bowed against him and moaned.

That's when she learned something very important about this man. Sex was the endgame for him. Or at least tonight it was. Maybe he'd been too built up or pushed too far by all the teasing she'd done on the dance floor, but he hadn't been exaggerating earlier.

He didn't do gentle.

One of his arms wrapped crossways over her chest, pinning her to him. The other hand held her hip, his fingers digging into her flesh while he pounded into her, leaving her no choice but to come into her climax. Tears leaked from her eyes with every pound of his hips.

He was so deep.

Perfect.

Hard.

Screams poured from her mouth as he took her right to the very point of euphoria. The difference between him and her ex: he delivered on his promise. With a final hard slap of his pelvis against her ass, she bucked and jerked against him, moving her hips, claiming the pleasure he offered.

With his final roar as he took his, too, he didn't only claim her body, he owned her soul.

Chapter 1

One year later…

In the west precinct of the Seattle Police Department, Joss O'Neil purposefully sat in the back of the briefing room, her mind far from the job. The epic one-night stand she'd experienced a year ago captivated her thoughts. Perhaps having wild sex in the bathroom of a nightclub hadn't been the classiest spot to give in to her desires. But the guy she'd met that night had given her the hottest sex of her life. She vividly remembered the way he'd touched her and how he'd made her feel. Wanted. Sexy.

Then life had happened, as had five months of the police academy and another eighteen weeks of field training. While that night hadn't been far from her mind during her training, there was a good reason that guy was at the forefront of her thoughts now.

Bedroom eyes stood at the front of the room behind a long table, addressing a group of ten police officers sitting in rows in front of him.

Maddox Hunt. Police lieutenant. Total badass.

From what she'd learned recently, he was also the resident heartbreaker. Or so she'd been told by her best friend, Emilia when she'd started in the west. Once Emilia had seen Joss drooling over Maddox, she'd said not to expect much in the way of getting a date out of him. Apparently, there'd been whispers around the station that Maddox liked his sex kinky and his relationships fleeting. But a guy with serious commitment issues didn't deter Joss—it sealed the deal. Then and now.

A relationship had been the last thing on her mind at the nightclub. Even a year later, she wasn't looking for anything long-term. She'd given six long years to Nick the prick, who'd then broken up with her after he found a better life in New York City. The blow had stung. She'd been hurt, devastated over the breakup. Nick had been her life for a big chunk of her high school years and during university, too. Most of all, she'd been angry with herself. When had she lost her backbone? Where had her voice gone? When he'd broken up with her, she'd sobbed like her life was over. *Barf!*

Never again.

Never again would she be that quiet woman who didn't think of her feelings first. Never again would she stay silent and not speak up for the life she wanted. Never again would she settle for a man who didn't touch her with the passion she deserved.

Leaning back in her seat, watching Maddox addressing the group, she remembered that she'd woken up the morning after the nightclub incident without a single bit of remorse. Even now, she didn't regret a damn thing. The filthy, dirty sex he'd given her that night had been all she was after.

Still, though, even after seven days of working for the Seattle Police Department, she had a hard time accepting that he was her lieutenant. When she'd been offered the job with the Seattle PD in the west precinct under the command of Eric Dalton, the police chief and a close family friend, she hadn't even considered that her one-night stand might be her superior.

Somehow, that meant she had to forget that everything Maddox did screamed *sex.* The way he moved like a tiger ready to pounce. The way he spoke, low and confidently. How his intense eyes watched her sometimes. It had only been one week of them working together, and already she couldn't take any more. Hell, her deprived vagina was silently weeping.

"You really have got to stop looking at him like that," Emilia whispered, dragging Joss's attention to her.

Joss leaned to the side. Coming closer to Emilia, she whispered, "It's near impossible when he looks like *that.* Couldn't he have gotten…I don't know…uglier in the past year? Seriously, I think he looks better than I even remember him looking before."

Emilia laughed quietly.

She knew Joss inside and out, and she'd listened to Joss endlessly gush about Maddox for the days following the one-night stand before the police academy had taken over their lives.

Emilia was two years older, with warm, hazel eyes and honey-colored hair that she usually wore in a bun—mostly because the job required it. They'd met five years ago because Nick was best friends with Troy, the guy Emilia had been dating and who she'd ultimately married.

"You also had three martinis the night you two defaced the bathroom," Emilia said with a sassy smile. "Maybe your head was a little fuzzy?"

"We may have christened the bathroom, but there was no defacing," Joss defended.

Emilia snickered, a hand over her mouth. "Maybe, but regardless, you're right. That guy…" She glanced toward Maddox standing at the front of the room and stared a little dreamily at him. "He's seriously *hot.* And if I weren't married, I would be *so* jealous that you got to touch him." She looked sideways at Joss, a sly smile crossing her face. "Okay, maybe I am a little jealous. But protocol is a finicky bitch, and that sexy beast is now your superior, so stop looking like you want to eat him."

"I don't want to eat him." Joss looked from left to right, glad no one sat anywhere near them. Most of her fellow rookies sat as close as they could get to Maddox. Not her. She didn't want to smell his woodsy cologne and feel all that sexiness wafting off him. "I only want to lick him and claim him as mine."

Emilia's light brows rose over her eyes. "You lick it. You bought it."

"Exactly." Joss laughed.

"Ladies."

Joss's lips snapped shut, and she jerked her head to the front of the room, finding Maddox with his narrowed eyes directly on Emilia. Which also wasn't a surprise. As much as she'd been avoiding Maddox, he'd been avoiding her, too. He never talked to her alone, and when he did look at her, there was so much distance, he seemed like a completely different person than the one she remembered. In the nightclub, he'd had heat in his eyes. Intensity. Now…*nothing.*

Heartbreaker, indeed.

That night, *blistering hot.*

A year later, *ice cold.*

His left eyebrow arched, and as it did, he said, "Is there something you would like to share with the rest of us?"

"No, sir," Emilia said, firmly shaking her head, fighting a smile.

Only then did Maddox look at Joss. "And you, O'Neil?" he asked curtly.

"No, sir, nothing to share."

The muscles in his jaw clenched twice before he looked away, allowing Joss to breathe again. He turned and addressed the group. "We've had a good week," he told the crowd, pressing his knuckles against the table in front of him.

She watched him closely, noting that he had a special way about him. He commanded a crowd in a way she hadn't seen before. People respected him. Trusted him.

That energy filled the space when he added, "And a good first week should be celebrated."

"Uh-oh, prepare to panic," Emilia whispered under her breath.

The mother of all curse words echoed in Joss's mind as Maddox calmly added, "Tonight I'll be hosting a barbeque in my backyard, as has been my annual tradition with my team." He straightened from the desk and crossed his arms over his thick chest, glancing from face to face. "Let me know if you aren't able to make it."

"I can't, sir," Emilia spoke up, raising her hand. "My shift doesn't end until midnight tonight."

"I'm sorry we'll miss you," Maddox said, again scanning the room. "Anyone else?"

In the front row, Tommy began, "My mother had surgery, and I need to be there for her..."

Joss leaned over to Emilia and whispered, "There is no way in hell I'm going there alone."

"Sadly, I think you are," Emilia whispered back.

Joss could barely stop herself from throwing herself at Maddox, and that was while she was in her uniform with a clear moral barricade stopping her. At his house? Out of uniform? With booze available? Oh, she was in big trouble.

Joss began considering every option to get out of this. Dammit, she'd never been a good liar. Usually, if she attempted even a little white lie, she ended up making a complete ass of herself and stumbling over her words. "Can't I suddenly be viscously sick and send him an email?" she asked Emilia.

"An email, Joss?" Emilia snorted, resting her arms on the table. "He'll know why you're avoiding him. Do you want to have *that* conversation with him? He's going to know that you're bailing because you two fucked like rabid bunnies."

"Oh, dear Lord." Joss groaned, dropping her head into her hands. It was bad enough seeing him for these briefings every day and having to pass him in the hallway. "I can't do this, Emilia." Joss lifted her head, glancing at her best friend. "You need to help me think of a way to get out of it."

Emilia paused, her eyes flicking up to the ceiling while she nibbled her lip. Only a second later, she shrugged. "Sorry, buttercup, I've got nothing. It'll be worse if you don't go. I know he said it like it's a choice, but it's not." She peered in Maddox's direction and shuddered. "And believe me, Maddox—with all that alpha broodiness—really isn't the type of guy to not call you out on it. I wouldn't put it past him to do it in front of everyone either. Is that what you want?"

"No, of course not," Joss grumbled, miserable. Sadly, Emilia knew him best from working alongside Maddox in the east precinct before transferring to the west. "I honestly don't know how I'm going to get through this."

"Hmmm…" Emilia pondered, tapping a finger against her lip. "Oh, I know. What about your mother? If anything can kill your raging hormones, it's your mom being there. Bring her."

"I wish I could." Sally O'Neil loved to talk. If her mother were there, Joss could be silent, while pretending she wasn't thinking very dirty things about her boss. "But my parents are still in Paris." Every year, they took a few months off to travel the world. Retirement life had its perks.

Emilia sighed. "Okay, well, that's a shame. Even your dad would help if he were around."

Joss nodded, knowing Emilia was right. Dad was a retired cop. He could talk shop while Joss faded into the shadows. It wasn't that she couldn't control herself around Maddox. Of course, she could. The problem was, she kept thinking she would slip up around him. Let him see how much she still wanted him, if he hadn't already seen it. And how awful would that be, considering he'd told her plainly: *this is a one-time deal*? Especially considering their night together had happened a year ago.

The last thing she wanted was to look pathetic and horny.

She focused back on Maddox, watching him talking to the others as they began to rise from their seats. His presence rattled her in ways she hadn't anticipated nor was prepared for. She was supposed to have forgotten him. That's what you did with one-night stands. You screwed and moved on. But it almost felt like they had unfinished business.

Sexy, unfinished business.

As the cops began leaving the room, Maddox's eyes met hers. Those intense, warm eyes held hers, and her breath became instantly trapped in her throat. The same butterflies that had whipped around in her belly a year ago returned. Heat flooded her, and warm wetness slicked between her thighs, making her panties feel *tight*. Energy seeped into the room so heavily, goose bumps rose on her flesh. And like she had that night in the bar, she felt *seen*.

"So, what are you going to do?" Emilia asked, snapping Joss's attention away from Maddox.

She blinked, rose, and tucked her chair under the table. "I'm going to go to that damn party." What other choice did she have?

"Atta girl." Emilia smiled and patted Joss on the back. "Put on those big girl panties with pride."

Joss snorted a laugh and followed Emilia out of the room, thinking to herself: *I secretly wish he'd rip those panties right off.*

THE WORKDAY ENDED uneventfully. It wasn't until later that night at the barbeque while Maddox was flipping the burger patties cooking on the grill that things began to look up.

From his spot on his large, redwood deck, he glanced to the reason his cock was semi-hard, and his balls had felt stuck in a vise grip all damn day.

Joss O'Neil.

She stood near his outdoor stone bar, chatting with two other male rookies who'd obviously taken a clear interest in her. He understood why. She mesmerized him the same way. Long, chocolate-brown hair. Light green eyes with gold flecks around the irises. Pouty lips that had once ravished him with blazing hot kisses. And a body with enough curves she felt like a woman beneath his callused hands. Maddox had liked that difference between them. His hardness to her softness was a contrast he enjoyed.

He wasn't entirely sure what it was about this girl exactly, but she pushed at all his basic instincts. Pursue. Claim. Protect. And as he watched one of the men place his hand on her arm and laugh at something she said, he fought against the desire to march over there and interject himself into the conversation, putting her focus on him. But he knew better. He never went back for seconds. Besides, she was now his subordinate, and touching her could put him in the line of fire for a sexual harassment lawsuit.

"That's her, isn't it?"

Maddox glanced left, finding Greyson Crawford, his college roommate, offering him a beer. Maddox took the beer, and Grey ran his fingers through his dark blond hair, his gray eyes pinned on Joss across the way. "Yeah, that's her," Maddox replied. Truth be told, he hadn't intended to tell Grey about Joss. That was until his foul mood lately had left him with no option but to explain.

While most cops at the party had loved ones at home, or even family to spend their weekends with, Maddox had Grey. Regardless that Grey wasn't on the force, his close relationship with Maddox meant an invite to events meant for cops. Sure, some cops didn't like an outsider in their midst, but Maddox welcomed the day someone said something to him about Grey's presence.

With the shit Maddox saw on the job, and what he'd seen some children go through in the foster system, he never mourned that his mother had left when he was four years old and didn't return. Nor did he feel bad about his father, John Hunt, who lived in a nursing home due to his worsening Alzheimer's. But when Grey demanded answers for Maddox's tense mood in a way only a brother would, Maddox had to oblige.

"I see what all the fuss is about and why this chick has you working out harder than you have in years," Grey said, finally glancing back at Maddox. "She's gorgeous."

"Those words don't do her justice," he admitted.

Joss was a woman of equal innocence and naughtiness. That was the sweetest type. His favorite, in fact. He recalled in vivid detail the way she'd melted under his hands a year ago, and that's what had been driving him crazy all week. He needed to get her out of his head. He needed to stop smelling her sugary perfume when she wasn't there. He needed to stop hearing her sexy-as-fuck moans when she came during his dreams.

Grey downed a big gulp of beer, watching Maddox closely. When he lowered the bottle, he noted, "I see by that twitch in your eye, you're still being the gentleman."

"My eye is not twitching," Maddox snorted, beginning to move the cooked burgers off the grill to the serving plate. Once he'd finished, he tossed on some more meat then called out, "Burgers up."

Grey silently watched the crowd, who, like vultures, claimed all the patties. Not until everyone was out of hearing distance did he continue. "Bullshit. You're twitching like a man who needs a fix."

Maddox couldn't deny that. He felt like an addict who was scrambling to put his life back together again. She was simply *there* in his mind. All the time. He'd jerked off every morning and every night—sometimes twice—since she'd come back into his life. "Regardless," he told Grey, tending to the burgers, "there are obstacles in my way. Very serious ones."

Grey barked a laugh. "And when has that ever stopped you before?"

Never. He took what he wanted when he wanted it. The problem was, he never conquered a woman a second time. Doing so could lead to an attachment. And he'd learned from his father that that never led anywhere good. "The last thing I need is a sexual harassment lawsuit," he said, offering up a concern Grey could understand.

"You're right, you don't," Grey agreed. "Though you could test the waters and see if she's looking for what you are. Perhaps she's trustworthy enough that something playful between you would be doable."

Maddox flipped the burgers then looked up and examined Joss grabbing a beer from the cooler. Her white summer dress highlighted her spectacular curves, enticing him to bend her over that cooler. The memories of her were vivid. How creamy her skin was, the way she moaned, the way she smelled, the way she tasted, he remembered it all. And so did his throbbing cock.

"It's risky," Maddox said, glancing back to Grey. "Too risky."

Grey grinned. "Which makes it even more fun."

Sounded great to Maddox, too. That was the problem.

While he tended to the burgers, flipping the ones needing it, he considered all the ways he could make this happen with her again and then rejected each idea. Besides the fact that their shared professional life was a huge obstacle, and even though he did have a feeling after working with her for a week that she was trustworthy, touching her again broke his one unbreakable rule: Don't screw twice.

Tension tightened the muscles across his shoulder blades when Grey, who was looking at the bonfire, asked, "So, these are your new rookies, huh?"

"Some of them." Maddox reached for his beer resting by the grill and downed a big gulp, scanning the crowd in his backyard. Some of his team sat around the bonfire, while others hung around the outdoor bar. When his father had gone into the home, Maddox had sold his bachelor pad and opted for the house that had been in the Hunt family for three generations. "Not a bad-looking bunch, are they?"

Grey's eyes zeroed in on Holly, the most recent rookie to join the team. "You are a lucky son-of-a-bitch, you know that, right?"

Maddox grinned, knowing why Holly drew Grey's attention. He loved blondes, and the curvier, the better. Maddox tipped his beer bottle toward Grey. "That might be true if I were allowed to touch. Which you well know I'm not."

Grey tsked, shaking his head in obvious disappointment. "You can't touch women who look like *that* and who come with their very own pair of handcuffs?" He glanced at Holly again, who was approaching the bar. "What a waste."

Maddox chuckled, tending to the burgers again, fully understanding Grey's point. A fondness for kinky sex was one thing Grey and he had always had in common. They'd even shared a couple of women once or twice throughout the years. There wasn't a fantasy Maddox had that hadn't been fulfilled. He made sure of it.

Though, over time, the show had eventually gotten old.

Grey went through girlfriends like he went through boxers. Maddox stuck to one-night stands to keep things interesting and to give him the distance he preferred. He'd never been a man who wanted one woman.

That was until Joss had walked back into his life a week ago.

Round and round his mind went. He'd stop ruminating about her for a second, only to start thinking about her again. He sighed and rearranged the burgers on the grill for even cooking. Somehow, she had gotten under his skin. Maybe it was how she'd melted under his touch. Or how she'd responded so beautifully to him. For the last year, he'd searched for the same high he'd gotten with her, only to be let down time and time again. Others didn't compare. Didn't even come close.

As the food on the tray continued to vanish, he knew he needed to put a stop to this, and he had to do it tonight. She controlled him too much. He thought about her too often. This was his test, and he couldn't fail. Surely, if he could stand being around her outside of work, he could gain control of the lust running rampant within.

With those thoughts on his mind, he gave the patties one last flip, then found Grey openly eye fucking Holly. "Please do your best to behave tonight," he told him sternly.

Grey slowly looked at him, one eyebrow arching. "And do you plan to behave yourself?"

"You know I have to."

Grey pushed away from the pole he leaned against and grinned. "Luckily for me, I'm not a cop, and I choose that sexy little blonde over there." He pulled on the hem of his shirt, straightening it, and strode off, eyes set on Holly.

Maddox shook his head, yet wasn't concerned. Years of friendship had taught Maddox to trust whatever Grey did. Even if he ended up taking one of Maddox's rookies home, she'd leave his house feeling respected and satisfied. If it didn't affect his job, Maddox didn't care who screwed, and he never understood why the police department frowned upon relationships between cops.

Life happened, and so did love. Why fight a natural thing?

"May I?"

Maddox turned toward the sweet, soft voice, instantly captivated by Joss's soulful green eyes. He went from semi-hard to rock-hard so fast, he fought off a groan. "Yes, of course. Please, help yourself." He gave her a gentle smile, hoping to hide the carnal thoughts racing through his mind, those of bending her over and thrusting himself deep inside her sexy, lush body until she was quivering her release. He cleared his throat. "Are you enjoying the party?"

"Very much so, thank you." She smiled, scooping up the burger onto the bun on her plate. "You have a lovely home."

The smile she gave him was so fake, it narrowed Maddox's eyes. He craved the realness he'd seen in her before. That's what had captured his thoughts over the last goddamn year. That's what was in his head every time his lips touched another woman. Their smiles weren't honest like hers. She'd appeared to hide nothing of herself, bared everything as if she didn't owe the world a damn thing. That transparency had mindfucked him.

He stared at her now, noting how she squeezed her plate tightly, knuckles turning white, telling him that she was doing her best not to shake. Another thing that had made his restraint even more difficult. She didn't hide how much she still wanted him. Her desire was there in her rosy cheeks and her parted lips and her deep breaths.

"So…um…thanks for the burger…and for the party." She lifted her head, and her light eyes met his.

The energy pinging between them was like a punch to his chest. His muscles tensed, breath halted. The softness, the yearning, the ache he so desperately felt, too, all crossed her expression, hardening him to steel. For a year, he'd forced himself to believe that he'd imagined this potent energy between them. That it was inconceivable to think their connection held this much power. Yet there it was, right there in front of him. Tangible. Intense. Real. His nostrils flared as he inhaled the sweet scent that had haunted him.

"Oh, shit," she gasped, breaking eye contact.

Without saying anything more, but not needing to because her subsequent silence spoke volumes about her desires, she scrambled away.

Maddox clenched his jaw muscles, watching the way she stiffly walked away. Fuck, he understood the need coursing through her. The same urgency pulsed through him. Could he trust her? He'd read the reports and the glowing recommendations she'd received. She didn't seem flaky or a woman out to screw over her superior.

Even if he could breathe again, the spell she'd cast over him wasn't broken. The addiction ran wildly out of control in the same way it had when he'd first met her on that dance floor. That's when he knew an undeniable truth.

This girl didn't only make him want to break his rules.

She made him want to abolish them.

Chapter 2

In desperate need of an escape and to breathe air that was far away from Maddox, Joss left the partygoers behind and strode along a lighted pathway next to the outdoor bar that led somewhere. Truth be told, it didn't matter where it led. Anywhere was better than being near Maddox's pulsing energy that made her mind a damn circus.

An hour. That's all it had taken for her to do what she'd sworn she wouldn't do—melt in his goddamn presence. She'd let herself feel all the passion he embodied and allowed herself to remember the way he'd made her feel that night at the bar. Sexy. Desirable. Alive.

Dear God, she wanted to experience all of it again. Over and over until she was sweaty, exhausted, and completely satisfied.

As she strode along the pathway, the chill of the breeze created goose bumps on her arms, and she hugged herself, rubbing them away. The voices behind her grew quieter, the relief she'd been looking for. She needed to think. She needed to put Maddox behind her. She needed to look at him like her lieutenant, not the man who'd given her the hottest night of her life. One she simply couldn't forget.

He seemed to be capable of that, always seeming so professional, so why couldn't she?

Careful not to slip on the rocky ground in her two-inch heels, she recalled how much she'd changed after that night in the bar. She hadn't been the same because she missed the way Maddox had made her feel, which made her regret agreeing to the one-night stand plan. Even if she didn't want a relationship, she for sure wanted to bone him again.

From time to time, she'd wondered if maybe it'd been the one-night-stand fantasy that had caused her mild obsession with him, but she knew that couldn't be true. She still felt drawn to him in ways she couldn't explain—an entire year later. Every night in those quiet moments before sleep took her, she thought of him…his touch…his passion…his rawness.

She rubbed her arms again, warming her skin, knowing he'd ruined her for any other man. No one compared. Sure, she'd tried to go on a couple of double dates with Emilia and Troy and Troy's firefighter buddies, but none of them had that something special that Maddox possessed. No one even came close.

Now, like some punishment, she had to be near him when all she wanted to do was forget him. Her career mattered, she reminded herself firmly. She had to get past this. She had put all her focus into finishing at the top of her class, both in university while she'd obtained her criminal justice degree and in the police academy to stand out from the rest. She couldn't fuck this up. Nor could she allow a sex scandal with her lieutenant to crumble her dreams of making detective in a few years. The last thing she needed was Maddox requesting that she transfer because of her inability to stop ogling him.

She heaved a long sigh when she discovered that the path stopped at a bench with a perfect view of Elliott Bay. The bright half moon lit up the sky, making the water glisten like black glass. She heaved an even longer sigh and dropped down onto the bench, staring out into the peaceful night. Off in the distance, lights sparkled off a couple of boats. Right as she glanced up to the starry sky, the sudden crack of a branch caused her to glance left.

Maddox stood at the end of the pathway a few feet from her, his hands shoved into the pockets of his pants. He wore a plain white T-shirt and jeans, but nothing about him was plain. His strong biceps, thick forearms, and powerful thighs standing out in the pale moonlight were all she could see.

Warmth began to flow rapidly through her veins, her nipples tightening into taut buds. She squeezed her thighs together, feeding pleasure to her clit. This was what he did to her. That simply. What no one else had done to her this past year. He harnessed something powerful that spoke to her on every level. He had the on/off switch, and she was basically just along for the ride.

He stared at her for a long time before addressing her. "Why did you leave? Is everything okay?"

God, she didn't want to have to say it. Her heart began to race, and her palms grew sweaty. "Listen, I'm sorry I looked at you that way," she said, lifting her chin and holding his stare. "I know it was wrong. It won't happen again."

He paused. Then, "You think I don't like when you look at me like that?"

She swallowed deeply at his implication and in response to the low tenor of his voice. The same warm, sensual tone she'd thought of every night since she'd first heard him speak. Her mind began to spin, her body yearning for him to come closer. "Do you?"

"Of course, I do," he murmured. "It tempts me to do things I shouldn't."

She blinked in surprise, butterflies filling her belly. "To be honest, that's not what I expected you to say."

"What did you expect?"

"For you to agree that this is wrong."

"This *is* wrong," he confirmed, beginning to approach her. Like a hunter stalking his prey, he closed in with large, unhurried strides. She rose, and the heat of his body encased her. "I'm aware of how complicated this is. I know that, professionally, I shouldn't touch you. It's incredibly risky. I also don't fucking care. Do you?"

She stared into the warmth of his eyes, instantly drawn in. "I thought you didn't come back for seconds?"

His left eyebrow arched. "Are you saying no?"

She considered him. The risks were real and true. Unavoidable. Yet with him close, being the guy she remembered from the club, wanting her in the way he wanted her before, those risks seemed small in comparison to the reward. "I want you," she whispered.

The side of his mouth curved, and he pressed the strength of his body against hers, letting her discover his erection. "It can only be tonight. One more taste to cure the hunger."

"Yes, only tonight, like a dream," she echoed his concerns, knowing the roadblocks between them. She, his subordinate. He, her superior.

"That's right, sugar," he murmured, sliding his hand across her lower back, pulling her into him, nice and close. "Like a filthy, dirty dream." He tilted his head down to her, his warm breath brushing across her lips. "A dream where the good girl wants to make some bad decisions."

"With the one guy who's very good at being bad." She knew his thing. After this, he'd bail again. Too many complications stood between them. Too many risks. Even now, voices from the party carried through the air, screaming *danger* at her. Anyone could catch them. At any minute. Her career would be tarnished as the gossip of them together spread.

Though the thought of being caught titillated her in the same way she'd been excited at the nightclub. Again, in Maddox's presence, she felt awakened and alive. Her blood pulsed. Her heart hammered in her ears. Her body ached to be claimed by him.

He dragged his mouth back over hers and whispered against her lips, "I've thought about touching you for the last week. I've thought about bending you over and taking what I want."

"Then take me."

He didn't need further invitation, his lips sealed across hers. It didn't matter that anyone could catch them. Or that he was her superior. She wanted him for tonight. She wanted to feel what she'd felt a year ago.

At first, his kiss was sweet, gentle even, lightly teasing. His tongue slid against her bottom lip until she opened for him. His mouth brushed against hers, his hands soft on her face. She moaned, a needy sound she didn't recognize, and pressed herself against the length of his body. A low growl rose from his throat as he cupped her nape and yanked her closer, deepening the kiss. His tongue dove into her mouth, stroking with a perfect rhythm, causing heat to flare. She wasn't thinking consequences when his hand left her face, traveling to her bottom where he ground her up against him. Her body instantly remembered *him,* her nipples puckering in anticipation, her sex becoming drenched.

She moaned again, the sound raw with desperation.

He grunted, low and deep, and then backed way, resting his forehead against hers, breathless. "I can't do this right. It's going to be quick and hard."

The air brushed across her overly sensitive skin, making her yearn for his rough touches. "Maddox," she whispered, not even recognizing the heady desire she heard echoing in her voice. "Please…"

He leaned away then and looked at her. His brows drew together as he cupped her face. "I like hearing you beg, sweetheart. Do it again."

"Fuck me. Please."

The side of his mouth arched in that sexy way it did. Eyes locked on her, he reached into his back pocket. The energy he tossed out into the world caused her clit to throb. No one had ever wanted her like this. Like he was starved for her. He looked so damn desperate to consume her; he made her want him just as much.

Her inner muscles clenched in anticipation as she watched him free himself and apply the condom. She was reduced to a panting mess of need before she was back in his arms. He lifted her slightly, carrying her behind a tree and into the shadows. She gathered her dress, lifting it over her hips, desperate for him to take her away. He pushed his jeans and boxer briefs down to his knees and removed her panties, quickly bunching them into a ball in his hands.

"You can't be loud," he told her, assisting her to lean against a boulder she hadn't known was there until she felt the large rock beneath her bare bottom. He grasped her leg and added, "We don't want trouble."

That was the only warning he gave before he tucked her thigh across his hip and entered her, right to the hilt.

She gasped, shocked at how he filled her. It'd been a long year since she'd taken a lover, and Maddox was so very deliciously hard inside her. She wrapped her arms around his neck, holding herself tightly to him. Every time he shifted his hips forward, she quietly gasped, and when he withdrew, her inner muscles squeezed to keep him deep inside.

"Christ, you're tight." He grunted, low and deep, shifting her leg higher onto his arm, his lips sealing over hers again.

Each swipe of his tongue deepened the kiss more until all her thoughts fled her mind, and all that remained was him and her, and the crackling heat between them. He pumped his cock, slowly at first, then faster and faster until her breath grew raspy. His skin never slapped against hers, the only sound was the faint sucking noise of his body entering hers, but she didn't need the force of his body banging against hers.

His cock was enough. All she needed. God, he was perfect inside her. Owning her. Taking her. Possessing her.

Pressure and weight filled her lower body. She broke off the kiss and dropped her head back, the warm air brushing across her face as he moved faster now. It all became too much, too intense. His body against hers flooded her with an unnatural heat, making her tumble into sensations only he could bring.

His hand suddenly slapped over her mouth, silencing the moans she didn't know were spilling out.

She lifted her head, finding his dark eyes pinned on her. "Fuck, how I want to make you scream," he growled.

His captivating eyes. His sculpted, sexy mouth. The intensity on his face. The pressure of his palm against her lips, forcing her silence. The thickness of his cock, filling her perfectly. His low and heavy breaths, consuming her. The voices carrying on the wind, reminding her of the danger of being caught…they all drove her higher. Until she couldn't take anymore.

"Oh, God, yes," she whispered beneath his hand, her inner muscles quivering.

His gaze smoldered. "Do that again, sweetheart."

The choice to convulse around him didn't belong to her, but she obliged naturally. She squeezed his shaft, climbing the cliff of euphoria. Everything about him drove her higher and higher. The way he looked at her, watched her with those hungry eyes. The way he held her like she wouldn't break, stretching her leg high so he could get as deep as he wanted. The way he filled her, taking her with abandon as if he couldn't get enough of her.

All those reasons pushed her closer to the edge, but it was his growl that sounded an awful lot like possession that sent her free falling. To be wanted so vocally gave her all she'd been missing. At whatever he saw on her face, his cock grew harder and bigger inside her. Tears leaked from her eyes as he pumped his hips a little faster now, a bit more out of control. His fingers tightened into a fist in her hair, his teeth bit his bottom lip, and when he thrust forward and groaned, giving a deep shudder, spilling himself inside her, she unraveled. She bucked and jerked against him until she rode out every single second of her climax.

Some time later, her mind returned to her, and she began to catch her breath.

"Even sweeter than I remembered, sugar," he murmured, slowly kissing her mouth until she found the strength to kiss him back. Only then did he slide his mouth from hers, gently placing butterfly kisses on her neck as she heard him zip up his pants.

Then she looked at him.

In the darkness, she watched him lift her panties. "Goddamn perfect." He brought the lace to his nose and inhaled deeply. She should be embarrassed, but his low moan of approval left no room for shame. "A small gift to remember you by, yes?"

She nodded, speechless.

He gave her that sexy half smile. Then, he was gone, as if her second taste of Maddox Hunt had all been a dream that she'd imagined while sitting on the bench staring out at the dark water.

Chapter 3

Maddox woke the following morning on edge. As his morning continued at work, things only got worse. From his spot behind his desk in his small office, Maddox glanced at the clock on his computer monitor: *11:00 a.m.* He sighed. This day had begun to annoy him. Seconds felt like minutes. Minutes felt like hours. While Saturday shifts went hand-in-hand with a cop's life, Maddox wanted to be anywhere but there. So far, all he'd done was reports, and all he wanted to do was Joss—in every dirty way he'd been thinking about since he'd gotten another taste of her.

Last night, he'd taken another bite of the forbidden fruit. He'd done so in hopes that he'd appease his hunger. Only problem? Touching her again made the fire for her burn even brighter. She hadn't been as good as he remembered. She'd been better. The way her body surrendered to him, heated for him so intently, responded to him so beautifully, caused him to want her again. And again. And again...until he extinguished the inferno between them.

He'd dug himself into a hole. Joss was an addiction he craved to feed, not cure. And that was a fucking problem.

"Hunt."

Maddox glanced up, and his back straightened like a steel rod as Chief of Police, Eric Dalton, entered his office. He froze in his seat as rapid thoughts blasted through his mind. Part of him knew he had this coming. He'd touched someone he shouldn't, and the chief would call him out on it. The stronger part of him said that Joss would never report him. She had far more to lose than he did, including her reputation. Maddox's job was already established. Sure, the scandal would be a blow to his career for a little while, but he'd recover. Joss? It wouldn't be so easy to repair the damage.

Dalton added, "Got a minute?"

"Yes, of course, sir. Good morning." Maddox rose, offering his hand, prepared to defend his personal life.

As the chief took the seat in front of the desk, Maddox studied him, getting a read on his mood. Eric was a tall man with a soft middle. The years had been tough on his face, and his deep-set wrinkles around his eyes and forehead were likely both from the long years of police work and the cigarettes Maddox could smell wafting off him. While Chief Dalton held a tough exterior, his light blue eyes were soft and trusting and were likely why so many Seattleites respected him.

Once the chief got settled in the chair, he said, "I hear you had a party last night to celebrate the new rookies."

Maddox paused, awaiting the reprimand. When it didn't come, he answered, "I did. The party went well."

Dalton gave an easy smile. "It's a good tradition that you do. Keep it up."

Maddox exhaled the breath he'd been holding and leaned back in his chair. The chief's posture was casual and laid-back, telling Maddox nothing had been said to him. He watched as Dalton ran a hand over his eyes, and on a hunch, Maddox offered, "We have some fresh coffee, sir, if you'd like a cup."

"It's that obvious, huh?" Dalton asked with a heavy sigh. "It's all right, Hunt. I've already had three cups. We have a a situation brewing in the east, and it kept me up for a good portion of the night last night."

Maddox noted the dark circles under the chief's eyes, and while he had his suspicions about what the trouble was, he wouldn't speculate. "Will the trouble impact us here in the west?"

"No, I don't believe so." Dalton rubbed his face once more and then lowered his hand. His eyes were troubled. "I'm assuming that you've heard the rumors circulating about Harvey Scott, the captain in the east?"

The department's rumor mill had been in overdrive lately. From what Maddox had heard, Harvey was an alcoholic who was spiraling out of control after the recent death of his wife. The police had been called twice after Harvey's drunken rage impacted the public. While Maddox hadn't been sure if the rumors were true, the darkness in Dalton's eyes confirmed that they were. Keeping his thoughts to himself, Maddox replied, "I'm not one to listen to the rumors, sir."

"That's good of you." Dalton crossed his legs, resting his arms on the armrest. "However, sadly, in this case, the rumors are very much true. Things are a mess over there in the east, and it's been an exhausting process trying to figure out which way to proceed."

Maddox had questions, of course. It simply wasn't his business to ask them.

Dalton's face twisted as he drew in a long, deep breath before continuing. "The captain is making a fine ass out of himself, and last night, it appears the media might have gotten wind of it."

"Not a good look for the department," Maddox offered.

Dalton snorted. "I imagine you're right about that. And I further suspect that no matter how much I'd like to give Harvey another chance, that right may even be stripped from me." Regardless of his words, the chief's eyes suddenly softened, and he stretched out his legs, crossing his ankles. "I'm sorry, Maddox, I didn't come here to unload on you. Tell me, how is your father doing?"

Dad and Dalton had worked together as beat cops for a handful of years back in the day. "Health-wise, he's doing well. His mind, however, is failing him."

"Alzheimer's, right?"

"Yeah, that's right." Maddox stretched out his fingers to avoid the fists that always came when talk of his father ensued. Speaking with others who knew the father Maddox had grown up with was hard. To watch a strong, proud man lose himself wasn't easy. "He has glimpses of his past every so often, but nothing more than that."

The chief looked troubled by this news, his expression tightening. "He doesn't remember you?"

"No, sir."

"Damn shame that is," the chief said, clucking with his mouth and shaking his head. "I'm sorry to hear that, Maddox. I know that being your father meant a lot to him."

"Thank you, sir. It is what it is, and truthfully, he's happy and spending his days surrounded by pretty nurses." Maddox smiled.

"There's always an upside to everything, I suppose."

Maddox agreed with a nod. He'd accepted his father's diagnosis after receiving it. There wasn't anything he could do to stop the way the disease ate away at his father's mind, so he'd made peace with it.

Now, when he went and visited his dad, Maddox played the part of support worker at the nursing home, instead of the son his father had raised. The reminder of everything he'd forgotten usually sent his father into a rage. So Maddox stopped reminding him.

Obviously sensing that Maddox didn't want to continue, Dalton shifted to a surprising topic. "I actually came by today to ask how Joss O'Neil's first week was?"

Maddox froze. "I wasn't aware that you knew O'Neil," he stated gently, not to overstep. "May I ask how you two are acquainted?"

"Her father used to be my partner. Didn't you know that?"

Maddox's heart rate began to slow, a connection forming that he hadn't expected. "No, I wasn't aware."

The chief paused as three rookies chatting loudly amongst themselves passed by Maddox's office. One look at Dalton and their mouths snapped shut. The chief chuckled, seemingly amused by the power he held over the younger generation of cops, before addressing Maddox again. "It's old news, I'm sure," he explained, pulling on the cuffs of his shirt. "We were partners during our thirties and early forties, a few years after I worked beat with your dad. Our families became very close during that time, and her father called me last night since they're traveling in Paris. He was concerned that maybe some of the staff would give her a bit of a hard time considering the connection I have to her family."

Maddox's jaw clenched tightly as he realized everything Joss had stacked against her. She was going to have to fight harder than most to get the respect she deserved because she was so well connected, and that was without having an affair with her superior.

"So, how's Jossie doing?" Dalton asked.

Jossie?

I'm a dead man. He took a sip of his coffee to gather his thoughts, set the mug down next to his computer's keyboard, and explained, "She's a good asset to the team. Clever. Fair. Hardworking." *Beautiful. Intriguing. Strong.*

The chief smiled. "She hasn't received any trouble, has she?"

"Not that I'm aware of," Maddox replied. "But I'm not sure she'd come to me if she had."

"What makes you say that?"

Maddox snorted softly. "Because I'm her superior officer, she's a rookie, and I'm a man."

"I suppose you're right," Dalton continued thoughtfully. "Although, word does spread quickly if anyone feels that someone is being treated differently." He paused, watching Maddox closely. Obviously, whatever he saw in Maddox's expression comforted him since he continued. "Regardless that there hasn't been any trouble yet, Joss means a great deal to my family and me. I can trust that you'll take care of her while she's here, Hunt?"

And there was the warning.

Maddox saw the threat in Dalton's narrowed eyes. Joss was clearly beloved by him. That's when Maddox knew the complication he'd thought he faced before was nothing compared to what he was up against now.

The thing was, no one dictated Maddox's life, not even the police chief.

Regardless of the mess he'd landed himself in, and even if a plan to move forward wasn't solidified, he stared into Dalton's eyes and made an easy promise, "Of course, sir. She's safe on my team."

—ᨓ—

AT THE END of his shift, Maddox had planned to go to the gym and burn off some steam. He'd questioned himself a thousand times when it came to Joss. If things went south with her, the risks were hefty ones. Earlier today with Dalton only reminded him that he walked on dangerous ground. Logic told him to steer clear of her. And yet, there he was. At her front door.

Now decided, he lifted his hand and knocked twice.

Not a second later, the door whisked open. The light from her living room spilled out into the night, and the remaining strands of his indecision evaporated. Tonight, she wore gray jogging pants and a purple T-shirt. Her hair was pulled back in a tight ponytail, and her face was fresh, without any makeup. When heat flooded him, swelling his cock, he knew he'd made the right decision to see her tonight. There was nowhere else he wanted to be than right there with her.

When she took him in on her porch, her eyes went huge. "What are you doing here?" she gasped, glancing behind him as if he'd brought people with pitchforks to get her.

Beginning to feel unwanted, he shoved his hands into his pockets and chuckled. "Is this usually how you greet your guests?"

She didn't laugh with him. In fact, she looked stunned, unmoving. She blinked twice. "What's wrong?"

"Nothing's wrong." He frowned. "I'd like to talk to you. If that's all right."

She blinked again. "Why?"

He began to narrow his eyes on her. "Joss, I want to talk to you. If you'd like me to leave, tell me to go, and I'll go."

"No, no, it's not that." She opened the door a little wider, the shock lessening *slightly* on her face. "You have me thinking that someone saw us last night, and now I'm being slut-shamed at the station. Please tell me that's not true."

"Believe me," he said seriously, giving her a measured look. "If you were being slut-shamed, I'd be dealing with that instead of standing here at your front door trying to talk to you."

"Oh, thank God." She sagged against the door, obviously relieved. When she straightened, her expression turned curious. "If you're not here because we've been found out, then why *are* you here?"

He paused. Then, "I've come to talk about us."

Now it was her turn to pause. "But I thought there was no 'us?'"

"There wasn't, but I'd like to change that."

She stepped away from the door, folding her arms. "Color me confused, but doesn't that go against your 'I don't date' policy?"

"Which is exactly the problem, isn't it?" He couldn't beat around the bush. Things needed to be crystal-clear. "I'd like to propose something to you that may work for both of us. I'd prefer to do that inside your house, instead of outside on your porch. May I come in?"

She watched him a moment, nibbling on her lip before she opened the door fully, letting him inside. He entered then moved into her living room. Her home was cute and quaint—much like the woman on his mind lately. Simple, but classy. Warm, and inviting.

Once he'd reached her couch, he turned around to face her and got right to the point of his visit. "Here's the thing. I want to explore what's going on between us a little more, if you're up for that."

She leaned against the living room's doorframe, giving him a cute, quizzical look. "I'm sorry, but I'm not exactly sure what you're asking me here. Last night was supposed to get me out of your system. Weren't you the one who said you don't date?"

"You're right, I did. I *don't*," he replied, taking a seat on the armrest of her couch and folding his arms, watching her carefully. "We wouldn't be dating."

"So you're suggesting something more in the way of friends-with-benefits?"

"That's right." Maddox needed to be careful, more careful than he'd ever been before with any woman. No broken hearts. Get his *fix*, sedate his craving for her. Then they could both move on. But the past had proven that it would take more than two quick fucks to fulfill him. He needed to explore her fully, enjoy her entirely. "What do you think of that idea?"

Again she nibbled her bottom lip, considering him. "Have you had a lot of these types of relationships?"

"No," he admitted, knowing full well what his admission implied, but there was no going back. To have her, he needed honesty and trust. And he wanted to have her again and again until he calmed this insatiable need. "I already told you, I never come back for seconds."

She hesitated. Then shook her head. "But you want thirds with me?"

"Yes."

Another pause. Her eyes searching his. "Why?"

He rose from the armrest and moved to her in two large strides. Her sugary scent engulfed him as he took her into his arms. He noted the sexy smile she gave him seconds before he sealed his mouth across hers to make a point. In the same manner she had before, she melted against him, going all soft and warm and meeting him with a passion that spoke to him on every level as a man.

There was a connection between them that was as rare as it was perfect. A connection that he'd tried to refuse yet one that had become stronger since he'd touched her again. A connection he needed to explore.

When he broke off the kiss and backed away, her cheeks were rosy, and her lips were pink and swollen. Her light eyes screamed *fuck me*. "That's why," he told her, dragging his thumb across her damp lips. "There's something here, no? Something that's a little bit curious and wildly addictive. But there are also risks. Risks that are very serious because of our jobs. I've made my choice to accept those risks. But you need to make them for yourself."

She blinked once, then her eyes became less heated and more focused. "I'm willing to take those risks, too, if you can promise that this thing between us doesn't become public knowledge."

His mouth twitched. "You think *I'm* going to kiss and tell?"

She didn't falter and shrugged. "Everyone has friends. I don't mind you sharing your life with those friends, but I want to make sure you trust them enough not to say anything. This"—she gestured between them—"getting out would be a big headache for me."

He parted his lips to respond and then shut them, stunned. A smart, strong mind was incredibly sexy. She threw him off his game a little. He'd expected to be the one worried that she would talk.

Regardless, he explained, "My close friend Grey knows about you, but considering our jobs," he added to reassure her, "and the trouble it would bring for us, I don't intend to speak of our relationship in detail with him or with anyone else. Do you?"

She walked around him and took the spot on the armrest where he'd been sitting earlier. "To be perfectly honest, I've already told Emilia every single detail about what happened between us."

Emilia was part of the police force. He didn't like that connection. "Even what happened at the barbeque?"

"Not yet, but I will." At his frown, she added, "She's my best friend, Maddox. We don't have secrets. But I can promise that she's also a vault. What I tell her will never get out."

The honesty between the two women left Maddox feeling uncertain. On one hand, he didn't known Emilia like Joss did. On the other hand, Emilia clearly hadn't told anyone about Joss and Maddox's one-night stand a year ago, so he put his trust into Joss now. "All right," he said, conceding. "If you trust her, then that's good enough for me." Besides, Joss had a lot to lose if this information got out, including her reputation. That meant she trusted Emilia a great deal. "Now, let's be very clear on this, all right? If you want out, you'll tell me, yes?"

She paused, watching him intently and then burst out laughing.

"Something funny?" He frowned.

"Sorry, but yes." She sighed away her laughter, her cheeks flushing pink, her eyes twinkling. "Has anyone ever told you that you're the biggest contradiction ever?" Her mouth twitched as she obviously fought more laughter. "Did you know that you have a reputation for being a heartbreaker?"

"Yes, I'm aware," he grumbled, not proud of that title. He never meant to break a woman's heart. He never made them any promises. But some women couldn't handle a one-night stand even if they originally said they could. Hence why this conversation was so important. "But do let me in on why me being a supposed heartbreaker is so amusing to you."

Her eyes still laughed at him. "From what I've seen of you so far, you seem upfront and honest, so I'm trying to understand how anyone could have misread you so much."

"And that's funny to you?"

She smiled. "What's funny is how serious you are about all this."

"I don't play games," he reiterated. "I can't give you a relationship, but I can give you an adventure. You need to be okay with that for us to proceed. I don't want to hurt you."

She rose then and moved to him, placing her hands on his folded arms. "You won't hurt me. I can handle a friends-with-benefits relationship with you. This is good, and if it ever becomes not good, I'll tell you."

"We're all clear, then? No misunderstandings?"

"Crystal-clear. Just sex. I got it." She gave a sexy grin, pressed herself against him, and practically purred, "So, about this *just* sex we're having. What exactly do you have in mind?"

"Something filthy, of course." He grinned, unfolding his arms to grab hold of her.

"Oh, I like the sound of that." She rose on her tiptoes, begging him for a kiss.

He ignored the offer, determined to say what he needed to. "We can start off slow—"

"No, Maddox, that's not what I want," she said, wiggling against him, inviting him to take her right there in her living room. "I don't want gentle. I don't want careful. I want what you've given me already."

He stared at her mouth and swiped his thumb across her parted lips. "And what's that?"

"Something raw and real. Passionate and wild."

He dropped his head, bringing his mouth so close to hers, he could feel her warm breath against his lips. "If that's what you want, then there's something you'll need to do for me."

"What's that?"

"Wait."

His grin rose at the surprise rushing across her features. When he walked by her, she called, "Wait for what?"

Once he'd reached the door, he grabbed the handle and glanced over his shoulder with a smile. "For the game to begin, sweetheart."

Chapter 4

Bright and early the following morning, Joss entered the station, passing by Maddox's office. Heat flooded her with no effort on his part. Maybe it was the intensity in him when he focused on whatever he was doing or maybe it was something else, Joss didn't know. Regardless, he looked hotter than ever before, and how *that* was possible was another thing she didn't know.

The more she thought about it, the more she wondered if it was because of the offer he'd made. Really, she'd never met anyone like him. So bold. Arrogant without being overly cocky. Demanding in the best kind of way. He simply knew what he wanted, took it, and made no apologies for it. She liked that about him. Perhaps that's what drew her to him.

She squeezed the strap of her bag and slowed her stride, getting a good look at him sitting behind his desk. One hand was behind his head as he stretched out his thick chest and talked on the telephone. She stumbled a little, and her shoe scuffed the floor. That's when his eyes met hers. Slowly, he lowered his hand, his posture stiffening.

A rush of energy flooded her. Exactly as it had last night when he'd come to her house. Her lower body pooled with heat, yearning for his touch…his hot kisses…and his dominating, powerful sex.

His eyes followed her, the seconds feeling like minutes. Regardless of the dangers of being with Maddox, he was not a guy to say no to—not that night at the bar or the night at the barbeque or when he'd offered her more last night. He delivered where Nick had failed. His touches brought out something in her, something new and refreshing and exciting and thrilling. Nick had always felt like he silenced her. Like he didn't want her to be who she was. The control Maddox possessed was the exact opposite. Somehow, his dominance and intensity freed her, making her feel like she was breathing easier. Making her happier than she'd felt in a while. And all he asked for in return was no attachment.

No mess. No emotions. Exactly what she wanted, too.

He finally blinked, the spell gone, and as fast as she'd seen his desire, his shields snapped into place and his expression hardened. She didn't take it personally—she understood, and she appreciated it, too. Police stations, like any workplace, could be rumor central, and her new job mattered to her. She'd worked hellishly hard to get where she was. The last thing she wanted was for others to think she'd screwed her way to the top.

Her eye contact broke when she moved past the door, and she exhaled the breath she hadn't even known she'd been holding. And in that same second, a firm grip latched on to her arm, yanking her sideways. "What the—" She was tossed into the station's family bathroom.

Emilia hastily turned around and locked the door.

Joss blinked, aghast. "You did *not* pull me into the bathroom. What if someone saw you, what in the hell would they think?"

"Whatever. No one saw me." Emilia waved her off, her eyes twinkling. "Besides, it's the only room where we know we won't be overheard." She moved to the sink and turned the faucet on all the way, then spun around and pointed a finger at Joss. "You banged him, didn't you?"

"Seriously?" Joss snorted, rolling her eyes. "By what you saw on my face as I walked down the hallway, you could tell that?"

Emilia scanned Joss over from head-to-toe. "Oh, hell yeah, it's *that* obvious. You have that glow. I know that glow. I saw it the day after you slept with him in the bar. So, spill. Every. Single. Detail."

Joss shook her head, watching Emilia lean in, practically salivating. "Yes, we banged. Yes, it was unbelievable. Yes, I'd do him again in a second, which before you say it, I know is a terrible idea considering the shitstorm that would rain down on us if the chief found out." Especially considering that Chief Dalton was a close family friend and he'd have no qualms about laying into her. "But this…Maddox and me…it needs to stay far under the radar. We're not dating. We screwed, that's it. So you can't say a word to anyone. Like, ever. Maddox could lose his job. My reputation is on the line." And her job mattered. Her father was a cop. Her grandfather had been a cop, too. Hell, she'd grown up surrounded by cops. She wanted to make them all proud. A sex scandal wasn't part of her career goals. "Did I cover it all?"

"Pfft." Emilia barked a laugh. "Not even close, honey. How did this happen? The last time we talked, I thought you were only joking about wanting to sleep with him again. Like, I don't want to be a Debbie Downer, but this could backfire—hugely—in your face."

"Yes, I know." Joss reached for Emilia's arm, giving it a squeeze. "I know what I'm doing, Emilia, but… "—she paused choosing her words carefully—"for so long, I always thought about what Nick wanted and how I could make him happy. Then I met Maddox, and that first night at the bar, things exploded between us. With him, it's all about me. I know the risks here. I'm well aware of them, but I'm sick of always doing the right thing or taking the careful route. We've talked, and I trust that he's going to keep whatever we do between us."

"So this is going to continue, then?" Emilia asked.

Joss gave a half-shrug. "Yeah, we've worked out a no-strings arrangement. It's just sex."

"Hmmm," Emilia said, nibbling her lips. "He does seem rather trustworthy and close-lipped. Just be careful, okay? Remember what I told you about him?"

Joss couldn't forget. That little reminder seemed ingrained in her mind. "He's broken a heart or two because he doesn't do relationships because of whatever fear or commitment issues he has."

"That's right, so you gotta remember that, 'kay?" Emilia moved to the sink and switched off the water. She turned back to Joss, softening her voice. "You're not built like him. You're a girl who loves love. You don't jump in and out of random men's beds."

Joss nearly argued with Emilia on that point. Maybe she had once been the girl who badly wanted to be in love. Double dates. Family Christmas celebrations. Walks in the park. She'd been the girl who loved all those things. But where did that get her in the end? Heartbroken. At least with Maddox, she already knew he was a heartbreaker. He'd drawn the lines clearly for her. All she had to do was not cross them.

Easy.

She placed her hand on Emilia's shoulder and smiled. "I love you for worrying about me, I really do. I know he's not a relationship guy, and I'm not looking for that either. What he can give me…that's what I want."

"Just sex?"

Joss grinned. "Just kinky, dominating, off-the-charts-hot sex."

Emilia laughed, her shoulders beginning to lower from their high position. "All right. Last bit of advice: Don't do it."

"Do what?"

She pointed. "Fall in love with him."

Joss snorted and turned the bathroom's door handle. "You don't need to worry about that. I can promise with total certainty that will *not* happen." Because as hot as Maddox was, as incredible a lover as he was, Joss knew better than to fall in love with the wrong type of guy, one with clear commitment issues.

When she swung the door open, she came face-to-face with Maddox.

"Oops," she gasped, taking a step back.

Stance wide, arms folded, narrowed eyes directly on her, he asked curtly, "Ladies, do you mind explaining why you are both in the family bathroom?"

Joss thought up every scenario from using the bathroom together to fix her makeup to changing her clothes, even if logically that didn't make sense since she wasn't holding anything.

Her lips parted to comment, when Emilia blurted out, "Sorry, sir, I asked Joss to bring me a pair of underwear into work because I"—she gave a shy smile—"sir, it's a ladies' problem that I'm sure you don't want to hear about."

Maddox's eyes narrowed on Emilia before he snorted, shaking his head. "Don't let me find you both in there again."

"Yes, sir," Joss said, nudging Emilia forward down the hallway. But, of course, she had to look, and when she glanced over her shoulder, she found Maddox's eyes not on their heads but on her ass. Soon, those eyes met hers and warmth filled her belly.

There was a whole lot of promise in them.

"Ooh, he looked pissed." Emilia laughed, dragging Joss's attention to her. "Good thing you can kiss up later."

Joss ignored that, refusing to *ever* talk about her and Maddox openly at the station. "Your period?" She snickered, nudging her shoulder into Emilia's. "That's what you came up with?"

"Nothin' shuts up men faster than period talk." Emilia grinned.

Joss laughed, though also wondered if Maddox would be the type of guy to buy tampons, or if he'd bail before she even got her period. Luckily, she realized, it didn't matter. Those were things guys in relationships did. She could buy her own damn tampons.

Emilia entered the locker room first, and Joss followed closely behind. There wasn't much to this space except two rows of lockers with benches, and some showers and toilets off in the corner of the room.

Joss approached her locker, hearing voices coming from the showers. She placed her bag down and opened the locker, immediately shutting it with a gasp.

"What's wrong?" Emilia asked, wide-eyed.

"Oh. My. God," Joss breathed.

"What, Joss?" Emilia bounced on her feet, attempting to open the locker. "What is it?"

Slowly, Joss cracked her locker open and remained assured that what she'd seen the first time was, in fact, there. She took another look around the locker room, ensuring in her state of shock that no one else had walked in.

Which they hadn't.

She carefully opened her locker, finding panties. Not just any panties, but her panties from the night at the barbeque, along with a note and a small black box with a pink ribbon on it. She couldn't believe that Maddox had risked coming into the women's changing room to put this in her locker. While she knew he probably had the staff's schedule on his mind and would know when the room was empty, it was still risky. Though she quickly realized that's what was so exciting and thrilling about Maddox. He took risks for the erotic experience. And hell, she appreciated that about him.

Ignoring the box for now, she opened the note clearly written in Maddox's handwriting.

8 p.m. My house. I'll be waiting inside.
Wear this for me.
—M

She glanced around once more as she placed her panties and the note into her bag, then she reached for the box. With quick fingers, she removed the ribbon, so afraid someone was going to walk in on them.

One look inside told her he'd bought her dark purple and black lingerie.

"You have *got* to be kidding me," Emilia mused, as Joss placed the box inside her bag and zipped it up. "He's not only gorgeous, and kinky as fuck, but he buys you sexy lingerie." Emilia sighed and rested a hand on Joss's shoulder. "Girl, my vagina is officially jealous of yours."

THAT NIGHT, RIGHT at 8:00 p.m. sharp, a knock sounded on Maddox's door. He exited the living room of his childhood home, sure his father had never imagined the sex that would unfold in this house tonight. Built in the 1920s, the house had an old-world charm with its covered porch and heavy columns in the corners. Inside, stacked moldings surrounded the doors and the windows, and on the floors were narrow, plank oak hardwood. Back when Maddox had sold his bachelor pad and moved his furniture in, he'd applied a fresh coat of earth-toned paint to the walls, keeping things light and simple. The only thing remaining of his father's touches were his dad's paintings and personal photographs on the walls. Those Maddox couldn't take down.

As he leaned against the living room's doorframe, the dark wood front door opened, and Joss appeared, wearing a short black dress and tall heels. The moment her eyes connected with his, they warmed with her smile. "Hi," she said.

"Hello." He grinned and winked.

That same craving for her filled his gut as her cheeks flushed while she took him in. Passion couldn't be taught, and Joss was off-the-charts passionate about him. He rather liked that about her. The way she melted for him and hungered for him was a combination he'd never seen in a woman before, which is what drew him in for more. Even now, he watched how her eyes grew heated as she glanced at his bare chest then down to the bulge in his blue jeans.

By the time her heated gaze rose back to his, his cock had hardened to steel. Tonight, he intended to satisfy them both. "Are you ready for the games to begin?" he asked her.

She shut the door then turned back to him with a smile. "More than ready. What comes next?"

He crossed his arms, watching her closely. "You undress for me, sugar."

She glanced from his staircase to his living room then back to his eyes. "You want me to take my clothes off right here?"

He nodded.

"While you're still clothed?"

"Yes, but leave your lingerie on," he told her, enjoying the way her cheeks flushed deeper. "Just lose the dress."

She watched him, and he saw the thoughts rushing across her expression, even if he couldn't hear them. Uncertainty showed in the nibble of her bottom lip. Concern was obvious in the furrow of her brow. Then he saw what he'd hope to see, the lift of her chin telling him that she'd pushed past all those insecurities to go after something a little more daring and exciting.

Keeping her eyes locked on his, she slowly unzipped her dress and then slid the straps off her shoulders. He followed her every move, letting her know how much he liked seeing her bare herself to him. Besides, he knew she'd get off on this as much as he would.

From the very first time he touched her, he'd wondered if she hungered for a new flavor where sex was concerned. Her flushed cheeks and dilated pupils indicated that he hadn't been wrong about her desires. She wanted to be sexy and sensual. And he wanted to create those moments where she could be.

Once the fabric had fluttered to the dark hardwood floor, she kicked her dress away and remained in her high heels. Only then did he approach her, slowly arrowing in on his his target. *Her.*

The closer he got, the more her sugary-sweet perfume infused the air. His nostrils flared as he inhaled her scent fully. While her tantalizing aroma twitched his cock, the sight of her wearing the lingerie he'd bought made his balls heavy with need.

Black and dark purple lace decorated her creamy white flesh while a garter belt sat perfectly around her hips, all leading down to thigh-high stockings. She was soft and curvy and lush and ready, and it was all he could do not to slam her against the door and bury himself balls-deep inside her.

"You look absolutely gorgeous tonight, Joss," he said when he reached her.

She gave him a sweet smile. "Thank you."

Needing a little taste, he took her chin in his hand and sealed his mouth across hers. He sensed her reach for him to deepen the kiss but he leaned away, ensuring they still had their minds straight enough for the conversation ahead of them.

Her cheeks flushed deeper when he titled her chin up, giving her the good once-over she deserved. She wore thick black liner atop her eyelids along with thick black lashes and purple shadow in a few different shades. "I've never seen you wear so much makeup before."

"It seemed fitting for tonight," she said with a soft smile. "Do you like it?"

He turned her head from side to side. She'd put in a lot of effort to look good for him tonight. "You're gorgeous, with and without the makeup." He dropped another quick kiss on her mouth before taking her hand. "Come. We need to chat a little bit before we begin."

As he strode forward into the living room, he noted the odd sense of trust that he could feel between them. She didn't doubt his motives and followed without hesitation. He liked that about her. She was like an open book, allowing him to read all the pages within.

When he reached his leather couches resting in the middle of the room, he motioned for her to sit while he moved to the stone fireplace. He needed distance, not trusting himself to be so close to her. Not with her looking like that and smelling as good as she did. Christ, he could only imagine how she tasted.

Sweet and ripe, he guessed.

To rein in those thoughts, he drew in a deep, stabilizing breath before turning to her. He found her sitting on the couch with her legs crossed like a goddess sprawled out for his taking. While the thought tempted him, he was intent on getting the night's activities started, and long ago, he'd been taught rules that were now engrained in his soul. Clear communication being one of them.

He moved to the coffee table in front of her and took off the black velvet blanket covering the antique tray.

Her mouth formed a perfect *O*. He smiled at her surprise, waiting for her eyes to lift to him before addressing her. "Tonight, I'd like to use everything I've chosen here. Any objections?"

She visibly swallowed then studied each object with great care, gnawing on her bottom lip. "You're going to use all of them on me?"

"Is that a problem?"

She looked from toy to toy before glancing at him again. "To be honest, I never imagined anyone would want to use all these on me."

"Well, I do."

"Why?"

He arched a brow at her. "Because I'm a filthy, dirty man, Joss."

She laughed softly, her eyes twinkling. "Obviously one who's unashamed of that fact."

"Why should I be ashamed?" he asked, moving back to the fireplace, giving her some distance to breathe and think clearly. "I like sex. The more erotic, the better. Sure, I could use my fingers or my tongue or my cock to make you come. Or even better, I could use all these lovely things I have laid out before you and then use my fingers, my tongue, and my cock and make you fucking explode. Which would you rather?"

"Definitely the latter." She grinned.

He chuckled with her, leaning against the fireplace and folding his arms before he got serious again. "This is meant to be fun. Even to be playful. If there is anything you don't like about what you see here, tell me. If I use anything on you, and you decide later you don't enjoy it, tell me."

"And you'll stop?"

"I'll always stop," he reassured her. "Say *yellow,* and I'll know I need to slow down. Say *red,* and I'll stop everything completely. But the point here is not to get you to level red. The point is to get you off and give you orgasms. All clear?"

"Crystal," she said, resting her hands on her crossed legs.

He watched her give the items one last look, seemingly a little more relaxed now, before he added, "You can also change your mind, you know. We can still take this slowly. Build up to more of what you're seeing here."

"Oh, hell no," she said with a firm shake of her head. "I'm in this. All the way."

"And you can stop this at any time, yes?" he reminded her.

She examined him and then smiled softly. "I trust you, Maddox. I know I'm safe here."

"Which is important. The more you trust me, the more fun we'll have." While she trusted him on a professional level, as her superior, soon, she'd know his kinky side fully and trust in that, too. "To be perfectly honest, and to reassure you, I'm not a sexual sadist. Whatever I touch you with, whether that be my hand or a toy, is for your pleasure, not for my enjoyment of causing you pain. Your orgasms are the endgame."

"Then what do you get out of this?" she asked.

"I get to control you. I get to do whatever I want to you, in all the filthy ways that turn me on."

"That's enough for you?"

If only she could see herself through his eyes. Sex with her wasn't ordinary. The high she gave him was only becoming more addictive. "More than enough, sugar," he reassured her.

Obviously, she believed him because she didn't press the matter more, and she glanced at the toys again. "So, in this little game of yours, what comes next?"

"You kneel for me."

With a sexy little smile, she rose.

She went to take a step toward him, and he said, "No, Joss." When her foot lowered back to the floor, her smoldering eyes locked onto him, he added, "Crawl to me."

For a few long seconds, she studied him, clearly wondering if he was serious. He stayed quiet, letting the silence and his firm look answer for him.

Slowly, she lowered to her knees, her chest rising and falling quickly.

He watched her closely and loved pushing the limits of a strong woman as she began crawling toward him. He didn't doubt that in her past, she'd had very vanilla sex with men who didn't ask what he'd ask of her. That's what he liked. He saw things in her that a vanilla man wouldn't see. A yearning to surrender shone within her. The willingness to submit under a dominant touch. The craving to experience something a little more intense, and definitely a bit wicked.

Sex in the nightclub. Sex outside. Rough sex. She liked pushing past the ordinary. He planned to exploit that knowledge and satisfy them both in the process.

And, of course, watching Joss go to her knees for him was a bonus.

He was a filthy, dirty bastard, after all.

Chapter 5

Oh. My. Motherfucking. God.

Never in her life would Joss have thought she'd crawl for a man. Maybe at first, the whole thing was awkward. Not now. Not with Maddox looking at her with those hungry eyes like he planned to fuck the living shit out of her, all because she'd done as he asked. Not with how she could see how much he liked watching her crawl to him. For those reasons and more, embarrassment simply never rose.

When she finally stopped in front of him, he dragged a thumb across her mouth. A trademark move for him that she'd begun to enjoy. "Be a good girl and take off my pants," he told her.

Intent to get him naked fast, she reached up and undid his belt and then unhooked the button of his jeans. He kept watching her with those intense eyes, stripping all her layers until he found the rawness of her. That's where he looked, right into her soul, and she let him as she pulled his pants down to his knees, freeing his erection.

After he'd kicked his pants away, he grabbed the base of his thick cock with bulging veins on the side. "Do you see what watching you crawl does to me?"

God, he looked so hard. "Yes."

Chin angled down, his eyes locked on hers, he stroked himself from base to tip and groaned. "Do you want my cock, Joss?"

She licked her lips, wanting to touch him. To taste him. "Yes."

"Where?"

She leaned up on her knees and ran her hands up his legs until her face was in front of his cock, offering herself.

He arched that left eyebrow, continuing to stroke himself. "I want you to tell me. I like hearing it from your pretty little mouth. Where do you want my cock?"

She paused. Then took his lead. "In my pretty little mouth."

"That's right, sugar." He gave her a sexy smile and dragged the tip of his cock across her lips, his full attention focused there.

When she took him into her hand, he removed his and she didn't wait—she slid him into her mouth and against her tongue. A ravenous moan she'd never heard before rose from her throat and filled the air as she tasted the saltiness of his pre-cum on her tongue and inhaled the musky scent belonging to him alone. She worked her lips over his shaft, up and down, while her hand followed. He groaned and ran his fingers gently over her cheek, never taking his eyes off her. There was something to his softness that she liked, because she knew it was purposeful, controlled even. Like, at any second, he could take over and make her body burn. Though for now, he was patient, letting her play.

Until she could tell that she'd teased too much, pushed too far.

His dark eyes greeted her as he stepped out of her reach. "I see that you're still good with your hands." He offered his hand, and when she slid her fingers into his and rose, he winked. "But I might just say you're even better with your mouth." He yanked her close and sealed his lips over hers. Strong and forceful, yet exactly what she needed and more.

When he broke the kiss and backed away, she was breathless and hot and wet and ready for whatever the hell he wanted. All of which he apparently knew by the smirk he gave her.

"Come, let's take this upstairs," he said, keeping her hand in his.

On his way out of the living room, he gathered the tray of toys and led her up the staircase to his bedroom.

Once inside, she found it to be much like the man, simple yet sleek. Light gray paint on the walls, along with a few pieces of metal art, a dresser with a TV on top and a king-size bed against the wall.

"Wait right here for me," he said, leaving her at the doorway.

He approached the bed, placing the tray on the nightstand, and she soon discovered that the sides of the bed lifted. She watched, curious, as he knelt on one knee and locked the plank of wood into place, revealing metal loops lining the wood.

In a matter of minutes, he had worked his way around the mattress. What had started out as a masculine bed now looked like a bondage table with a big mattress in the middle.

"Did you build this?" she asked, watching his back muscles flex to perfection.

He locked the final plank into place and then glanced over his shoulder with a nod and his sexy half smile. "Do you like it?"

"It's…" The craftsmanship was impeccable, truly. The wood was stunning with all the knots and colors throughout. "It's really quite impressive, and I'm a little amazed that you spent this much time on something used for sex."

"I imagine after tonight you'll understand why I spent so much time on it, and you'll appreciate that I did." He chuckled, obviously knowing a secret she didn't, while he returned to the tray on the nightstand. There, he picked up the black rope that appeared softer than any rope she'd ever seen in a hardware store. "Come here, sugar."

Her heart raced as she moved to him, but she wanted this. For so long, she'd had a boring sex life. Maddox offered her adventure, and she wanted to dive in, giving him the control to show her all the things she didn't know.

When she reached him, he gently took her arm and began wrapping her wrist as he explained what he was doing in a soft, gentle voice. "The knot I'll use is one I can release in seconds if you don't enjoy the sensation of being bound. All you need to say is *red,* and the rope will be gone. Understand?"

"Yes," she whispered, suddenly feeling warmer than before. The rope was soft but strong, like a man's firm hands, keeping her safe and yet eliciting danger. She studied Maddox and quickly decided that it was *him* that brought the heat, not the rope itself. It was the way he touched her, so skilled, clearly he knew exactly what he was doing. By the time he laid her on the mattress with both wrists wrapped in rope cuffs, her chest rose and fell with her heavy breaths.

Silently, he continued binding her wrists to the bed, and as the minutes drew on, the silence became daunting. He was so serious, so focused, so intent, all kicking up her heart rate in anticipation. *What comes next?*

The answer came a second later when he broke the silence. "Down the road, when trust is cemented between us, we can look to binding your ankles, too."

She rolled her eyes and frowned at him. "I told you I could handle—"

"Did you roll your eyes at me?"

The firmness in his voice made her rethink her answer. "I would say yes but I'm thinking that would be the wrong answer, so let's go with no."

That left eyebrow lifted. "Now you're lying to me?"

She gave him a quick smile and dropped her head back against the pillow. "All right, so I'm going to stay quiet and not roll my eyes since, apparently, that makes you huffy."

"Probably a good thing since if you do it again, we stop and you go home."

She jerked her head up off the pillow, finding his eyes as stern as his voice. "You would do that?"

"Disrespecting me because I'm thinking of your best interests and safety is a dead stop to this game."

She watched him for a moment, and found that answer instilled a whole lot of trust. "Point proven. Carry on."

"Oh, sweetheart, I intend to." He chuckled and winked, the playful nature to him returning as if it had never left.

Once he'd finished with the second binding, hooking the rope into the metal loop, she was tied tightly to the bed and unable to flee. He moved away to the tray again for only a moment then returned to her. Darkness fell over her eyes as a blindfold was settled into place. There was nothing but her heavy breaths and heart rate hammering in her ears until she heard a *click*…and another *click*. A lighter, maybe?

"Anything too tight? Or uncomfortable?" he asked, running a hand over her stomach until he reached her panties and tucked them to the side of her sex.

"No," she replied, her voice husky even to her ears.

"Tell me if that changes. Or say, *red*? Clear?"

"Crystal."

"Very nice," he commented, sliding his hand back up her body until he slid her bra beneath her breasts, exposing her taut nipples to the warm air.

Then he was gone.

Her breathing deepened, a sense of worry speeding up her heart rate. His chuckle came a second later. "You enjoy the sense of danger, yes?"

"Yes," she admitted. They both knew it was true. She liked the sense of getting caught by someone. She also liked not knowing what was going to happen next and that right now, at this moment, she had no control over anything. Of course, it wasn't logical, maybe even a little naïve. Yet Maddox was right—she was drenched, more turned on than she'd ever been in her life.

Maybe that was why he'd chosen to bind and blindfold her. The thought ripped from her mind as he cupped her pussy with pulsating squeezes, and she clearly soaked his hand.

"Gorgeous," he murmured before his hands were gone, and she felt the cold void of his absence spill across her.

She listened carefully, waiting for him to return. Only silence greeted her. Until his fingers slid over her body again, feeling different this time, holding more power, more passion even. He began touching her…*truly touching her* in ways she'd never been touched. He clearly liked caressing her, stroking her, fondling her, maybe even got off on it. She didn't doubt his cock was as hard as steel because she could feel his arousal in his hands. Her chest rose and fell with each of his sweet soft caresses, as her mind slipped further away, becoming lost in *him.*

"Very, very pretty," he murmured, squeezing her sex again before giving it a light tap.

She moaned at the contradiction of his touches. Sometimes, soft and gentle. Other times, hard and firm. Always perfect. She turned her head from side to side, desperately trying to catch her breath. There was a pause. A long enough pause that she began to wonder where he'd gone and what he was doing there.

Luckily for her, she didn't have to wonder long, as balmy liquid dripped onto her torso. She gasped and arched into the warm sensation, the rope pulling on her wrists. Each slide of the liquid heat warmed beautifully across her skin. Unable to stay still, she writhed against the mattress, falling into the heady sensation she equated to a warm bath.

Then the warmth was gone.

Silence.

Her heavy breathing and soft moans were the only thing she heard. The only thing she could understand. Until his touch came again, as he slid his hands up her thighs, and the warmth of his touch slowed her breaths. His hands weren't soft like before. They were rougher, more demanding, as his touch traveled higher up her body, removing some wax as he went. Once he'd reached her breasts, he tweaked her nipples, pulling on the tight buds until she was arching into him, begging him to pull harder, to give her *more.*

Silence.

She wiggled against the mattress, so wet, soaking for him to fill her, stretch her, own her. "Maddox," she whispered, unsure if she could take more. Handle more of him.

The wax answered her, landing right on her breast, and she heard his reply. He wasn't finished with her. Not yet. She moaned as the warmth was a little hotter this time, landing directly on her nipple.

Silence.

That's when she heard the click and the buzzing sounds of the vibrator she'd seen on the tray before her clit awakened under its pressure. She whimpered as more wax fell along her body right above her pussy, drawing all her attention to where he played. She moaned relentlessly now, not caring how desperate she sounded, not caring that she'd never been so loud in her life. She arched up into the vibe, rubbing herself against it.

She needed *more.*

Her fingers clenched into fists when the vibe suddenly sped up to a higher speed. Beneath the blindfold, her eyes rolled back into her head and she groaned, losing herself in her body being pleasured in ways it never had before. That's when she felt something along her mouth, a soft tickle.

"Open for me, sugar."

She parted her lips and he slipped a votive candle inside. Her mouth shut, holding tight, and she began breathing heavily from her nose. She wanted to thrash against the pleasure but the candle in her mouth kept her still, as did his hand on her neck.

She couldn't moan. She couldn't move. The buzz on her clit tickling in all the right ways, pleasuring her perfectly. Her fists were tight, her ass was up off the bed, her climax right…*there.*

Then, the mattress dipped down on her left, and the candle was pulled from her mouth. Maddox placed his hand on her pelvis, pinning her to the bed and pressing the vibe harder against her.

"Come, sweetheart."

And Lord, did she ever.

She thrashed wildly against the bed, screaming against the heat and intensity she couldn't control.

The next few minutes were a blur as she felt drunk from the pleasure. But soon, the vibe was turned off and the blindfold was gone and she saw *him*. Naked. Damp with sweat. Hungry with need. His dark eyes locked onto hers, intense and gorgeous, while he waited on his knees in between her spread legs, his condom-covered cock standing up, ready to take her.

She quivered from the power that only he produced as he leaned his hard body atop hers. He pressed himself against the wax covering her and slid his hands up her bound arms to grab her wrists, holding her tightly. He stared deeply at her as he entered her, making it as personal as a man could make it.

Slowly, he began shifting his hips, his cock sliding perfectly in and out. She watched him closely, too, seeing the way his attention moved from the ropes at her wrists to her face to her mouth to her breasts. He leaned on one arm, massaging her breast, sliding the remainder of the wax off and tweaking her nipple.

The strength of his body against hers, matched with his thick shaft stroking her inner walls, flooded weight into her lower half. She was so sensitive. Too sensitive. And as he began thrusting faster, his pelvis smacking against her engorged clit, her orgasm rose with no warning.

There, in the safety of his body against hers, in the sensations that he built to the highest peak, was where she lost herself again. His brows drew more and more together, the focus in his face becoming more and more intense as she squeezed him. Her arousal spread out between them, and she couldn't be ashamed over how wet she was because he thrust harder, more hurried and urgent. Until he'd claimed all of her, taking her as high as he could take her. Only then did he drop his head into her neck, hold her bottom in his firm hands, and give a low grunt as he bucked and jerked his pleasure.

In his strength, her teeth clenched, toes pointed out, as euphoria didn't glide over her—it *crashed*, sending her drowning in sensations until she lay boneless, breathless, unable to move even a pinky finger. She whimpered and quivered beneath him, knowing she hadn't only been fucked by him, she'd been owned.

He continued to blanket her, unmoving, catching his breath for many minutes until he eventually groaned, his breath tickling her neck. "Christ, you come so hard and sound so fucking good. You're making me blow far sooner than my pride likes."

She chuckled, stretching out her fingers, the rope still tight on her wrists.

He kissed her warm, sweaty neck, then rose and had her released from the headboard within seconds. Somehow, he ended up on his back, and she lay in his arms while he removed the rope cuffs. "This was a taste of what I can offer you. You can take what we had here and leave. Or you can accept this little game of ours and take more." That left eyebrow lifted. "Decide."

The decision was an easy one, and she answered within a split second. “More.” She lifted her head off his sweaty chest and stared at him right in the eyes. “I want more.”

His sexy half smile returned. “Then more you’ll have, sweetheart.”

Chapter 6

Two orgasms later, the sheet beneath Joss had been changed. She'd been wiped down, and at some point, Maddox had ended up back in the bed next to her. She couldn't recall all the steps that had gotten her to being cradled in his arms, only that she was glad she was. Warm and comfortable, she lay tucked into his side, his chest slowly lifting and falling beneath her cheek with his relaxed breaths.

He'd been silent over the passing minutes until his fingers began to trail over her hip and he asked, "If I asked you something personal, would you answer me?"

"Of course." She rose a little higher on his chest, resting her chin on her hands, getting a better look at him. She found his eyes…they were guarded. "What's on that mind of yours?"

He tucked an arm behind his head. "How many lovers have you had?"

Not the *personal* question she'd anticipated. "Why do you want to know?"

He gave a gentle smile. "Call me curious."

She thought about avoiding the truth, not sure what he'd conclude from her answer, but she figured…*what the hell?* "Two. You and my ex-boyfriend, Nick."

"Just two?"

She considered him, trying to get a read on his thoughts. His emotions were very much in check, leaving his face unreadable. "I'm not sure if I should be offended that you sound surprised. Do I seem easy to you?"

"Easy?" His expression turned clearly thoughtful. "No, not easy, but willing and eager."

She paused. Then, "Is that a good thing?"

"For me?" His eyes heated, his voice thick with promise. "Yes."

She examined him again, trying to figure him out. Usually, she was good at reading people. But this guy had a very strong shield up, keeping her out.

Before she could say as much, he smoothed the lines along her forehead and asked, "Was the other man like me?"

"Like you in what way?"

He shifted then, moving onto his side with his arm still tucked under his head. "Did he have a particular fondness for kinky sex?"

She noted how the blanket rested at his hips, showing off the hard, beautiful lines of his body before answering him with a snort. "I think Nick only knew two sexual positions."

"Hmmm," Maddox said, his eyebrows furrowing.

"Why does that seem to bother you?"

"Bother me?" He chuckled softly, shaking his head against the pillow. "Joss, why would it bother me that your ex-boyfriend was clearly a boring fuck? While I suspected you hadn't had much experience with the kinkier side of sex, it does make me curious how you made such a big jump. You went from one lover to having a one-night stand in a nightclub to now being tied up and fucked by me."

She could see his point. "Well,"—she recalled what had gone through her mind when she'd met Maddox at the bar that night—"after Nick and I broke up, I guess I was looking for something a little crazy and wild."

"And you're sure you're still looking for that?"

The concern on his face made her laugh. "You know, you can really stop worrying that I'm suddenly going to wake up and realize that I can't handle a sexual relationship with you. To be perfectly honest, wanting to date a guy that has clear commitment issues and who doesn't want to date me isn't in my relationship goals."

"It's amazing how you do that." He snorted a laugh.

"Do what?" she asked, tracing the curve of his six-pack.

"You speak as if you have nothing to hide."

She half shrugged, running her finger over his squared chest. "That's because I don't have anything to hide with you. For a long time, I hid my feelings with Nick, always trying to make him and the rest of our family members happy. With you, and because of our arrangement, I don't have to hide anything because I don't need to make sure you're happy."

He watched her finger move down his abs before looking into her eyes again. "And that's a good thing?"

"That's a *really* good thing," she confirmed. "For the first time ever, I feel like I can be myself."

"Well, then, I'm glad you feel that way." He looked to the ceiling again with a smile, then shut his eyes. "I find you…refreshing, so keep being yourself."

She smiled, too, even if he couldn't see it.

Right as she moved to lean her head back against his shoulder, he asked, with his eyes still shut, "Is Nick also why you're so determined to stay single?"

Back to this again? She wasn't sure why he kept focusing on her love life. Shouldn't he stay far away from this subject? "Shouldn't you be happy that I am single?"

"Of course, I am," he said, glancing at her with soft eyes. "But you're not like the other women I've been with. You're…" His eyebrows drew together, "You're a little too sweet, a little too real, a little too honest. You seem like a relationship girl, more than someone who's just looking for sex."

She smiled at the compliments he gave, and she supposed she could see why women became attached to Maddox. "I'm single because I don't want a boyfriend."

"Is there a reason for that?"

"Because I've been there and done that, and I don't want to do it again right now."

"You seem pretty certain of that." His brow arched as he tucked the fallen strands of her hair behind her ear. "Did this guy hurt you?"

"Yes. Horribly."

Something flashed across his eyes then, and she grinned, unable to help it. "You'd better stop looking at me like that, or I'm going to start believing that you're actually capable of caring about someone."

He jerked his gaze away, staring once again at the ceiling. "I never said I couldn't care about someone. I said I couldn't give what most women want."

"Well, I had what most women want, and then it ended in tears and heartbreak and wasted years."

He gave her a quick look. "What did he do to you?"

"Oh, you know, broke up with me," she said with a dry laugh. "At that time in my life, it seemed like the worst thing that could have happened to me. Now…well, now things are different, of course."

"There had to be a reason for why he ended things."

"I wanted a simple life in Seattle. He wanted a fancy life in New York City. I know that doesn't seem like a big deal, but to me, it was. I gave him six years of my life and was totally wrapped up in him. I thought we'd get married. I planned on it, going so far as to look at bridal magazines and keep articles and stuff. My future had him in it. Then he took away the life we'd built together, and I unraveled."

"You don't look all that beaten up about it anymore," Maddox commented.

She smiled, proud of that. "Because I'm not beaten up about it. I don't miss him, if that's what you're wondering. Of course, it took some time, but I realized how much of myself I'd given to him when he didn't deserve it. How his dreams mattered over mine. How I had honestly considered leaving everything behind to go to New York with him, all to be someone that I wasn't. Honestly, it bordered on pathetic."

"Why pathetic? Obviously, you cared for him."

"Because he didn't want me in New York with him."

"Oh," Maddox muttered.

"Oh." She laughed softly. "Apparently, I wasn't fancy enough for his new lavish lifestyle. Which he told me when he broke up with me on the telephone."

"Ouch," Maddox said with a frown.

She gave a firm nod. "Which is exactly why I'm not broken up about Nick anymore. He's a prick, and I'm lucky to not have wasted more years on him than I did."

"Well, from my point of view, the relationship made you strong," Maddox said, brushing his fingers across her cheek. "You're incredibly put-together, which makes you different. I'm not used to being with girls like you."

"What are you used to, then?"

"Girls who say they're fine with a one-time thing and then hunt me down afterwards. Girls who think they can change me."

This she had to know. "What kind of girl do you think I am?"

His eyes locked onto hers intensely. "A girl who sees me for what I am and is okay with it."

She wasn't sure why that one line brought so much emotion between them, but it did. His eyes were heated. She felt warmth slide within her, too. But she reminded herself that emotions didn't belong between them. Maddox wasn't hers to figure out, and that was refreshing. It didn't matter what was going on in his head. She liked his company. She liked his brand of sex. The rest didn't much matter. "Well, to answer your original question of why I'm single," she added to put an end to the entire conversation, "I think what most women want out of a relationship is highly overrated."

He gave her his sexy grin before shutting his eyes again. "And that, Joss, is the sexiest thing you've said all night."

She laughed, but then she began wondering over him. "All right, you asked me something, so if I asked you a personal question, would you answer?" She cleverly used his words back on him.

"Depends." His mouth twitched. "Shoot."

"Have you always been so kinky?"

His eyes opened then and turned his head against the pillow. "No, not always. At one time, I was a teen that would've fucked anything that breathed on me."

"Like most teenage boys, I suspect."

He nodded with a smile. "It wasn't until my early twenties that I was introduced to kink."

"Introduced, in what way?" she asked hesitantly.

He shifted on his side again, the blanket inching it's way lower off his torso. His gaze fell to her breast, and he began tracing her nipple. As the bud hardened beneath his touch, he said, "What I did to you tonight, she did to me."

She shivered as warmth pooled low in her body, his tickling touch circling her areola being a tease of something more to come. "I can't even picture that, to be honest. You being tied up and not in full control seems so unlike you."

"It is unlike me now, but it wasn't back then." His finger travelled slowly around the curve of her breast. "Back then, I had no idea what I was doing." His eyes lifted to hers, and they smoldered, as he added, "What twenty-one-year-old kid does? You're still figuring yourself out."

"That's when you got into all this? At twenty-one?" At his nod, she sorted through a hundred questions. "Do I even want to know how old the woman was?"

"Thirty-four."

"Of course, she was older than you," Joss said with a laugh. "Let me guess, your professor, right?"

He shook his head, sliding his fingers down the center of her chest to her belly button.

"Doctor?" she asked.

"No."

"Therapist?"

His eyes snapped to hers, and he frowned. "Definitely not."

"Well, then, who was it?" she said. "Because I know it has to be something scandalous."

He laughed easily, dragging his fingers back up her torso to her neck, then sliding them across her lips. "Sorry to disappoint you, but it's not that exciting." His eyes followed his fingers as he caressed her shoulder. "I met her while working at a bar as a bouncer. She was a bartender there."

Joss shivered as the heat from his touch caused her pussy to dampen with need, but she managed, "And this woman taught you about kink?"

"That's right," he murmured.

God, his voice got low and throaty, and she was finding it hard to concentrate. "So, what happened? Did you date?"

"No, we didn't date." He slid his fingers back down over her ribcage to her nipple again, where he circled her areola. "I told you I don't date seriously. We fucked for a few months."

"Ah, I see," she commented. "I'm not the only one who you were with more than once?"

"She was the only other one," he said with a measured look, "and that was back in my twenties."

Interesting point, which Joss decided not to look too deep into. She reminded herself that's what she liked about Maddox. He didn't want her to figure him out. No messy emotions. Bliss. "Then you ended the relationship?"

He nodded.

"Why?"

The side of his mouth arched then, and he climbed on top of her, sliding in between her thighs. "Because I decided I wanted to be in control."

Joss's heart rate kicked up, having all that man and muscle pressed against her. He blanketed her in the most spectacular way. "And she wouldn't let you be in control?"

"It's not what she wanted."

"So that was it?"

"That was it."

And that was the end of the conversation, too.

His mouth sealed across hers, and by the time he deepened the kiss, she'd forgotten the remainder of her questions. He grabbed the blanket off her, tossing it to the side, and slid an arm underneath her. She squealed as he flipped her over onto her knees.

Behind her, he wrapped an arm around her middle, lifting her, until her back pressed against his chest and his hand massaged her breast. He lowered his head into her neck and inhaled deeply. "You smell like a sugar cookie, did you know that?" His nose slid from the base of her neck all the way up to her ear.

She wanted to respond, she did, but she couldn't. All she could do was shiver at the strength at her back. At the feel of his lips. At the gloriousness of his hand massaging her breast.

"It's the most incredible smell," he added in her silence.

When he began nibbling and licking and scraping his teeth across her neck, she couldn't be still in his arms any longer. She wiggled against him, wanting more of his touch. Obviously, he heard her plea since his hands moved to her breasts and squeezed tightly, working over her until he pinched her nipples. She moaned with each perfect tug, which turned into a hiss as one of his hands cupped her sex. He teasingly squeezed her pussy, and she unabashedly swayed her hips, rubbing her sex against his hand. "Please," she begged.

"Please, *what*?"

"Please touch me."

"Like this?" he murmured, stroking her engorged clit.

She leaned her head back against his shoulder, reveling in the warmth building within. "Yes. Like that."

"Oh, but I think we can do better, don't you?" He dragged his hand from between her thighs up her torso to her mouth where she parted her lips, and he slid his fingers against her tongue.

With his fingers now soaking wet, he returned to them to her swollen clit. Like her own personal vibrator, he worked the bud fast, back and forth, pinching, swirling, bringing her higher. She began gasping and trembling, desperate for him to give her more. "What do you want, Joss?" he demanded, voice hard.

"Your tongue," she rasped.

He pushed her forward, sending her facedown onto the mattress. She grasped the sheets beneath her hands as he pulled on her hips, angling her bottom high in the air. Heat flooded her as he spread her bottom, opening her in ways no man had ever exposed her.

Then he hesitated, and she knew by his groan and the way his fingers tightened on her butt cheeks that he studied every inch of her. She'd never felt more vulnerable, and that rawness soaked her pussy in need. Her fingers clenched around the bed sheets when his tongue found her sensitive flesh, and she moaned and arched against him. He licked from the top of her sex right to her puckered hole, and back again. Over and over, he stroked and sucked her folds, teased her clit, and licked her slit. He never stopped, always driving her higher, until she began shifting her hips, boldly rubbing her sex across his mouth, needing more.

"Maddox…" she begged, not even knowing what she begged for.

He grasped her hips and then flipped her onto her back. She arched against the mattress as his mouth sealed over her clit. The stubble of his facial hair tickled against her inner thighs, seconds before his mouth covered her clit again and he sucked…*hard.*

She grabbed his head between her legs, holding him tightly to her. He teased and swirled and tickled the bundle of nerves until she fought for breath. Until she was unable to stay still, no matter that his arms were locked around her legs, holding her to him. She rocked her hips, gyrating against him, and he released one arm, pinning her with the other to the mattress. A rough moan escaped her dry throat as one finger entered her. Then another. He stroked her in perfect rhythm, while his tongue flicked her clit.

Pleasure roared through her, causing her chin to angle up and her muscles to seize, when suddenly his mouth popped off. His body then pressed against hers, and he sealed his lips over hers. She smelled herself on his mouth, as he angled his hand so that his palm connected with her clit. She tried to arch into the pleasure, but he thrust his free hand into her hair, pinning her.

All she was left to do was embrace the intensity that she had no control over.

Right as she began to quiver, he freed her.

"Give me what I want."

She unraveled, exactly as he requested. Her toes pointed, body frozen beneath the strength of his, and she free fell into the pleasure only he could offer. Ripple after ripple, she rode the waves of climax. And then she relished the satisfaction thereafter that only he could deliver.

When she began to catch her breath, he kissed away her whimpers and cupped her sex until the pulsating climax lessened. Then he brushed his mouth across hers in a whisper of a kiss. "I gave you a beautiful orgasm, didn't I?"

"Yes." She tried to slow her heart rate.

He lifted off her, leaning on one of his arms, and arched that brow of his again. "I do believe I deserve to be thanked, don't you?"

She chuckled, sure he was joking. When his firm expression greeted her, she realized he was dead serious. She had some hesitation, yet at the same time, she thanked a waiter for a good meal. Maddox had feasted on her to perfection, making her feel far more amazing than any waiter would. She leaned up and pressed her lips against his. "Thank you for my orgasm."

When she leaned away, power flared in his eyes. "Thank you for my orgasm, *what*?"

She lifted her head off the bed again and kissed his strong mouth, knowing precisely what he wanted by his authoritative tone. "Thank you for my orgasm, sir."

"Pretty little things from a pretty little mouth." The tip of his tongue slid across the edge of her bottom lip. "Keep talking like that, Joss, and I might think you're perfect."

She threaded her hands into his hair, holding him close. "Keep touching me like you do, and I might think you are, too."

Chapter 7

The next morning, after leaving Maddox's house late the night before, Joss woke up happy and satisfied in her bed. She had spent the morning running errands and then enjoyed an afternoon of shopping with Emilia. By the time she entered her condo minutes before 5:00 p.m., she was glad to be home and unlocked the door with a smile. Sure, her yellow-brick house in the Fremont neighborhood was tiny, being only eleven hundred square feet, but it had an awesome private, brick patio out back. She also never had to cut her grass, or shovel her driveway the once or twice a year the city got snow.

Once Emilia had followed her inside, Joss shut the door and dropped her purse onto the small table by the door. She was so ready to enjoy a few hours of girl time before heading into the night shift. Of all the shifts, the night shift was her least favorite and the hardest on her body, but when Tommy needed a couple more days off due to his mother's surgery, how could Joss say no?

As Emilia kicked off her shoes, she asked, "So, then, after he went down on you, you left?"

Joss laughed and shook her head, unzipping her boots. Her best friend had been stuck on Joss's sexy night for half an hour now. "Yes, I left." She moved past Emilia and headed toward the kitchen at the end of the hallway. "I'm not sure why this concept is so hard for you to understand. He rocked my world. Then I kissed him goodbye and went home to sleep."

"But did he say anything before you left?" Emilia asked, right on Joss's heels as she moved to her black countertop.

Joss grabbed two glasses out of the cupboard then turned back to Emilia with a grin. "He said, 'Thank me for your orgasm.'"

Emilia's eyes widened and twinkled. "And you thanked him?"

"Of course, I did. It wasn't that hard. Nick never made me orgasm. Not once in the entire time we were together. The only time I got off was when I helped him. I will happily thank Maddox until I'm blue in the face if he keeps doing all the things he's doing."

Emilia blinked. "Then what happened?"

"He kissed me silly, slapped my ass, and sent me on my way."

"Jesus Christ, that's so hot." Emilia sagged against the countertop, fanning herself.

Joss burst out laughing. "Right? He's like an erotic dream come true." She approached the fridge and took out the jug of iced tea and set to filling their glasses. "I honestly wouldn't have believed a man could breathe passion like a dragon breathes fire, but Maddox does. It's like sex pours out of him. I've never seen anything like it. He's filthy and dirty, but it isn't creepy, it's just fucking sexy."

Emilia's mouth twitched. "Maybe we should introduce Maddox to Troy." She put down the grocery bag containing the cupcakes they'd picked up at the bakery on the corner. "Seriously, I need some of this excitement and orgasms in my life."

"Oh, yeah, I can only imagine how that will go. 'Hey, Troy, meet Maddox. We think he should teach you a thing or two about sex.'" She laughed, placing the cap back on the jug. "Could you imagine?"

"Well, no," Emilia said with a shudder. "Troy would never forgive me. But still, maybe I should go get lingerie or something."

Joss waggled her eyebrows. "And maybe some rope, too."

"Oh my God." Emilia burst out laughing, grabbing the box of cupcakes out of the bag. "I'm not sure we're ready to take things to that level. Right now, I'd be happy with a spank or two."

Joss returned the iced tea jug to the fridge, realizing how much she liked that Maddox was at that level. She didn't think there was anything wrong with what Emilia had. She and Troy were perfect for each other, and Joss knew they had a good sex life and a very loving relationship. But explosive, mind-blowing, rock-your-fucking-world-apart sex, Joss was sure they probably didn't have that.

Once Emilia had placed two cupcakes on a plate, Joss followed her into the living room with the iced teas in hand, and Emilia asked, "All right, so tell me…do you just have sex and leave, or is there cuddling and talking, too?"

"We cuddled and talked a little last night."

"And that's not weird for you?" Emilia asked, taking a seat on the couch and placing the plate on the wooden coffee table. "To be honest, I can't really picture you being so okay with something so detached. You're always so open and honest."

Joss dropped down next to her friend, placing the glasses down next to the plate while she pondered. Last night, Maddox had questioned her reasons for sleeping with him. Now Emilia did, too? Why couldn't everyone get on board with the idea? "We're not detached necessarily," she explained. "It's simply different than what I had with Nick. Sure, it's a little out of the ordinary in terms of us not calling ourselves a couple or doing normal 'couple stuff,' but it's a partnership nonetheless. He gets something from me, and I get something from him."

Emilia's eyes tightened with concern. "You sure that's enough for you?"

"For now, it's enough for me." Joss settled against the couch and tucked her legs up underneath her. "Yes, I could go do the whole online dating thing and maybe meet someone. Hell, maybe I'd find my forever guy. But honestly, I don't even have the energy to go on dates. You know how it is. Most of the dates would end with you calling to save me so I could bolt."

Emilia smirked, tucking one leg underneath her. "Okay, but seriously, how much fun would that be? I'd come up with some of the best excuses to get you out of a bad date."

"I'm sure they'd be hilarious," Joss agreed. "But if I've learned anything from the break-up with Nick, it's that I need to think more about myself than anyone else. So, sure, Maddox and I are unconventional, but it's fun and exciting, and I'm okay with things being casual."

"But what if they get serious?"

"They won't."

"How do you know that?"

Joss laughed. "Because, Emilia, he doesn't date. End of story."

"All right, fine. I'm going to accept what you're telling me as truth." Emilia picked up her cupcake and licked some icing off the top before asking, "I guess the one question is: Does Maddox make you happy?"

"Maddox gives me orgasms, and *that* makes me happy." Joss hesitated, rethinking. "Honestly, he's actually kinda sweet and thoughtful in a way that isn't thrown in your face. He keeps asking me if I'm okay with our arrangement, like somehow he thinks he's corrupting me."

"He is, isn't he?" Emilia smiled, taking a bite of her cupcake.

"Yes, but I'm aware of it," Joss countered, trying to get Emilia on the same page. "Everything is out in the open and so clear that there can't be any misunderstandings."

"Well, there is that," Emilia said, wiping the crumbs off her mouth.

Joss looked down at her cupcake with chocolate sprinkles on the plate but wasn't ready to eat it yet. "I know this isn't like me, Emilia, and maybe it's all crazy, but he's exactly what I need right now. There's something about him that's so carefree and wild. He doesn't live by normal rules. There're no expectations there. I don't have to worry about things getting confusing and messy because I know he can't give me a relationship."

Emilia placed her cupcake down and frowned. "Good point, but I think that's what usually scares off women."

"I'm sure it is, but I'm not that girl."

Something crossed Emilia's face that Joss couldn't quite place. Concern, maybe? "Aren't you worried that you'll start liking him?" she asked gently, licking some icing off her finger. "I know he's being all upfront and honest, and while that makes him a decent guy, what if you fall in love with him?" She gave a knowing look. "I mean, from what you say about him, I imagine it would be pretty easy to do."

"Maybe, if things were different. But they aren't, and emotionally, he's completely unavailable. He keeps telling me over and over again that he doesn't date, and that sex is all he can give me. How do you fall for a guy who won't let you in at all?"

"And he doesn't let you in?"

"He's cautious about what he says. Careful, for sure. The second I get too deep, he brings on Alpha Maddox – Sex God to stop the conversation."

Emilia chuckled, taking another bite of her cupcake.

"I know you're worried about me, and I love you for it," Joss said with a smile, squeezing Emilia's forearm. "But he's not a guy you fall in love with. Lust, oh yeah, I'm all over it. But I've already loved someone who didn't love me back. Why would I willingly go into that again?"

"I suppose that's very true," Emilia conceded. "I guess you never know, the unimaginable could happen and he could fall head over heels in love with you, and you could live happily ever after."

Joss reached for her cupcake and laughed. "Now that is a true fantasy if I've ever heard one."

"Why a fantasy?" Emilia nibbled her cupcake with a frown. "You're beautiful, smart, and clearly someone he hasn't been able to forget. Don't overlook the fact that he wanted more of you, too."

Joss pondered before deciding not to look too deeply into it. She couldn't go there. Not even once. She couldn't ever cross that emotional line and examine why Maddox did the things he did. Hell, she simply didn't want to. No strings. That's where her happiness lay. "He came back looking for more because we had incredible sex together."

"Are you sure that's all it is?"

"Very sure. That's all he can give me." She peeled back the wrapper on her cupcake and, before taking a bite, said, "He's clear about that, Emilia, and I believe him." She swallowed then added, "Besides, sleeping with him is one thing. Dating him would complicate everything. First, one of us would have to transfer to a new division to avoid the conflict. Then, there would need to be a whole lot of explaining from Maddox about how he'd gotten involved with me in the first place. Not to mention, I'd likely have to lie to ensure that he didn't face suspension." Her head hurt even thinking about it. "It's a mess that I don't want, and I can only imagine he doesn't want it either."

"Yeah," Emilia said, licking the chocolate icing off her finger, "but sometimes, relationships are messy before they get all neat and tidy. All I'm saying is that you're both taking big risks here. Him, professionally. You, emotionally. I guess I'm wondering why either of you would take such big risks just for sex?"

Joss nearly allowed herself to fall into that train of thought, wondering about all the emotional intricacies, before she stopped herself. "Because the sex is amazing," was the only answer she felt needed to be said.

Emilia gave a look like she didn't believe Joss and lifted up the final piece of her cupcake. "Well, then, here's to many more emotionally unavailable orgasms and sexy secrets."

Joss laughed. "Hear, hear."

MADDOX HAD PLANNED to head to the gym for his usual workout after his shift ended. Tonight, he opted to take a run later in the evening on the Burke-Gilman Trail. An invite from Grey's mother, Anne Crawford, wasn't something he could decline. When he'd arrived at the Lake Washington south shore mansion belonging to Grey's mother, he found Grey waiting for him in the kitchen with a cold beer in his hand and one ready for Maddox. Anne was nowhere in sight, nor was

Grey's sister, Riley. The house hadn't always been so grand or modern, but it had been a house handed down in Grey's father's family for generations. The Crawfords had renovated the home years back when Grey was at the University of Washington.

"Are you seeing Joss again tonight?" Grey asked, taking a seat in the chair across from Maddox at the kitchen table.

Maddox shook his head and leaned back in his chair, raising his beer bottle to his mouth. Before he took a gulp, he said, "I decided tonight I'd much rather see your pretty face."

Grey snorted. "No, really, you've already ended it? I gotta say, I'm surprised. You seemed to enjoy this one, more than any of the others."

"I do enjoy her," Maddox admitted, placing the bottle back down on the natural wood table. He hadn't intended to tell Grey much about Joss, but being his closest buddy, he knew he'd have to tell him that she was still in his life. "And, no, it's not over. She's taken on a couple of night shifts. I'm seeing her again on Wednesday."

A perk of his job was to always be on the day shift, but it annoyed him—and his greedy cock—greatly to not see her for the next couple of nights. She'd been in his thoughts all day today. Before the idea could arise that he should text her to somehow squeeze in a quick visit, he stopped it. Surely, he could go a couple of days without seeing her again.

"Well, that's a pity," Grey muttered, reaching for his cell phone in his pocket and giving it a quick look before glancing at Maddox again. "Though, it's good to see you're keeping this one around for longer than a night."

"Don't get your hopes up." Maddox paused as the front door opened and closed. "You know this won't last long."

"Such a shame that is, though..." Grey fired off either a text or email before he gave Maddox a knowing look. "I thought this one might be different. You've got a certain sparkle in your eye."

"My eyes are not sparkling." Maddox frowned.

Grey placed his phone back down on the table and smiled. "Oh, sure they are. They're like twinkling stars in the sky."

Maddox snorted, lifting his beer to his mouth. "Fuck off, Grey."

"Language," Anne said, entering the kitchen, giving both him and Grey a look. "Haven't I taught you boys better?"

"Sorry, ma'am." Maddox narrowed his eyes at Grey before rising and kissing Anne on the cheek, Grey laughing the entire time. "You are looking lovelier than ever, Anne." She was the mother every kid wanted. There wasn't a day that Maddox came over when there weren't fresh cookies in the cookie jar. "Did you get your hair done?"

"Just yesterday." She patted her short, shiny, dyed silver hair. "I'm not sure I like the style."

"It's beautiful." Maddox smiled. "Don't change a thing."

"Suck up," Grey whispered beneath his breath.

"Ignore him," Anne said, taking Maddox's chin in her hand and looking at him intently. "You look happy. This girl who is making your eyes sparkle, she must be good for you."

Maddox sighed and gave Grey, who was now grinning from ear-to-ear, another glare. "Thanks a lot."

"You're welcome," Grey said with a firm nod, glancing back to his cell phone.

"Tell me about her," said Anne, drawing Maddox's attention to her while she frowned at Grey. "Greyson, don't make me tell you again. Put that cell phone away. It does not belong at the dinner table."

Grey's sigh was even deeper than Maddox's as he tucked his phone into his pocket. "Yes, Maddox," Grey said, lifting his head. "Do tell my mother all about the apple of your eye."

Maddox turned to Anne, who awaited his answer. Christ, he couldn't lie to this woman. She'd been so very kind to him over the years, inviting him into her house for every holiday and for any celebration after his father went into the home. The Crawfords were the closest thing he had to a family now. "Her name is Joss O'Neil. There isn't much to tell because we're not serious."

"Maybe you should be serious with her," Anne said, moving into the kitchen toward the stove. "If she's causing such a kerfuffle in your life that Greyson is commenting on it, she must be special."

"She's not causing a…*kerfuffle,*" he corrected gently, returning to his chair. "She's a very nice young woman who I'm getting to know."

"Yes, Maddox," Grey said seriously. "Maybe you should make this relationship a little more serious."

When Anne turned toward the cupboards and grabbed some bowls, Maddox flipped off Grey before Anne glanced back to them.

Grey chuckled.

Maddox focused on Anne and said, "Whatever you've cooked smells delicious."

"It's beef stew. I know how much you love it." She began scooping the stew out into the bowls before returning to the table and placing his bowl in front of him. The twinkle in her eye told him he wasn't getting off that easily. "There must be more you can tell me about this young lady. Grey has been a bachelor for so long now—"

"It's been a month, Mother," Grey muttered.

She shot him a little glare, hands on her hips. "A month that you're not finding yourself a beautiful bride who can give me cute grandkids."

Maddox grinned and reached for his spoon, glad Grey now had his turn.

Anne tsked. "Don't look at him like that, Maddox." She shook her finger at him, and Maddox wiped the smile off his face, as she added, "Just because I didn't give birth to you doesn't mean I don't expect the same from you. I don't care which of you gives me grandkids, I want them, and before you all turn forty would be much appreciated."

Maddox smiled softly, feeling bad for her. He'd never give her what she asked for. A wife? Children? *No.* That domesticated life wasn't for him. But Anne was sweet to include him in the conversation. "You always have Riley to make those dreams happen for you."

"She's only twenty-seven. She still has time," Anne continued, moving to the stove to scoop up some stew for Grey. "Tell me all there is to know about Joss."

When she returned to the table, placing Grey's bowl in front of him, Maddox obliged her. "She's a cop, too, and sweet like you. I'm sure you'd adore her."

Grey picked up his spoon. "That sounds like you plan to bring her over to meet Mom."

"Oh, yes, what a wonderful idea," Anne exclaimed, taking a seat next to Grey after fetching herself a bowl of stew.

Maddox heaved a sigh and shoved some beef and potatoes into his mouth to avoid a conversation he didn't want to have. It wasn't like he was some fucked-up guy that didn't understand *why* men liked commitment. Of course, he got it. That lifestyle simply wasn't for him. His father had shown him what love and commitment could do to someone. He remembered the sadness his father had carried for many years after his mother left. Maddox didn't want that type of headache in his life.

To change the subject, Maddox asked Anne, "Have you been enjoying the Bridge Club still?" She'd only recently become a member after she'd decided one of the women at her knitting group hated her.

"Very much so," Anne said, blowing on the stew on her spoon. "The ladies were so very welcoming, and we're all going to see a musical this weekend."

"That's great to hear." Maddox smiled, happy for her. Grey's father had died ten years ago from a heart attack. The man had smoked a pack of cigarettes a day and didn't watch what he ate. It wasn't a big surprise to anyone when he died, even if he did pass away in his fifties.

"So, more about this woman…" Anne pressed.

Maddox frowned down at his bowl. Weren't they done with this? "I'm afraid there's nothing more to tell."

"Are you seeing her often?" Anne asked.

"No."

"He's lying to you, Mom," Grey stated with a full mouth. "He's seen *a lot* of her recently."

Maddox lowered his spoon into his bowl and glared at the shit-stirrer. Payback would be a bitch.

Anne didn't pay any attention to Maddox's glare and said in her sweetest voice, "I'm sure she's already madly in love with you."

"Actually"—he softened his expression when he addressed Anne—"she isn't." That's what he liked about Joss, even if he still felt a smidgen of concern when it came to that subject. She seemed too good, too sweet, too full of heart to be a woman not out to find love. He trusted that she knew exactly what she was doing, and he only hoped that it didn't come back to bite him in the ass later.

"You must be wrong," Anne said, fixing the flower brooch on her purple sweater. "How could she not fall head over heels for you? Maybe she needs to hear you say you love her first. You know us ladies like a confident man."

"Mother," Grey muttered, scraping up the remainder of stew in his bowl.

Anne gave Grey another look and then said to Maddox, "All I'm saying is, maybe it's about time you make this woman a little something more than a fleeting romance."

"Please," said Grey, rising and pushing his chair under the table before picking up his bowl. "Maddox only believes in *fleeting romances*."

"Don't listen to him." Anne rose and came to Maddox's side. She placed a hand on his shoulder, giving him a warm smile. "Do not become a man who ends up alone." She pinched his cheek, giving him her cutest grin. "You're too charming and handsome for that."

He didn't respond, not having a suitable response. While Anne moved back to the stove and turned it off, he stared at her back. He *was* that guy. He liked being alone. He liked life uncomplicated. That wasn't something he could change about himself.

"Believe me, Mom," Grey added, scooping some more stew out of the pot. "He's going to be that old guy whose most beloved thing is his recliner."

Maddox snorted. "You know that I'm already in love with my recliner."

Grey glanced over his shoulder and grinned. "You're right, I do know that."

"I wouldn't speak too soon, Greyson," Anne admonished, pinching his cheek now. "At the rate you're going, you'll be sitting in the chair next to him."

Maddox barked a laugh.

Anne always did get the last word in, and it was usually the wisest.

Chapter 8

The following days were a bit of blur, with Joss taking on two night shifts. By late afternoon on Wednesday—and after three cups of coffee—she began to feel normal again. She drove through Seattle's busy downtown, tapping her fingers against her steering wheel to the beat of the soft rock playing through her radio.

When the car in front of her slowed, her cell phone rang from her purse resting on the passenger seat. She contemplated not answering it. Though she quickly thought better of it as she glanced away from the taillights of the car in front of her to her car's dashboard touch screen, seeing both that it was 4:00 p.m. and that her parents were calling for their weekly chat.

With everything that'd happened lately, she'd forgotten about their call. For a second, guilt crashed over her in a thick wave until she let herself off the hook. She was on her way to Maddox's, and lately, he seemed to steal up all the space in her mind. She rolled to a stop at the red light, her windshield wipers rhythmically sweeping away the steady rain, and she clicked the button on her steering wheel, enabling the Bluetooth. "Hello."

"*Bonjour*," Mom quipped.

"Oh dear Lord," Joss said with a laugh. "I seriously hope you don't try to speak French in front of others." Knowing her mother, she'd walk around with a dictionary in her fanny pack.

"Of course, I do," Mom defended, an obvious smile in her voice. "Besides, my French isn't that terrible, is it?"

"Yes, it's completely horrible. You shouldn't try it at all," Joss joked.

"Leave your mother alone," Dad interjected, playfully defending his wife. "She sounds lovely, and people seem to understand us."

"Well, that might not be totally true," Mom added. "I think they feel sorry for us."

"There is that," Dad mused.

Joss smiled and watched the pedestrians stride by the hood of her blue Jetta. Some with umbrellas. Some getting soaking wet and not seeming to care much about the rain. "How's Paris?" she asked.

"So romantic," Mom said with a dreamy sigh. "You must come see this place, Jossie. You would love it."

"Maybe one day," Joss said, not sure exactly when that day would be. First, she lived and breathed becoming a police officer. Now she had a job to think about. Besides, trips were expensive, and she never liked taking a handout from her parents. They'd both worked hard. She wanted them to live it up, not spoil her. "Are you still sightseeing?" She stepped on the gas pedal, slowly getting back up to speed.

Mom answered her. "That's all we've been doing. There's so much to see here. We've been around to see some lovely churches, the Louvre Museum. Tomorrow, we're doing the Seine river cruise and lunch at the Eiffel Tower."

"Man, that sounds amazing."

"Beyond amazing," Dad agreed.

Joss smiled, glad for them. Her parents deserved these trips of a lifetime they took every year, and she was proud they'd killed their bucket list instead of sitting at home spending their days around Seattle. "Make sure to take lots of pictures so I can see it all when you get back."

Dad said, "We're posting some to Facebook tomorrow. Have you been following us on there?"

"Yep." *Sort of.* Work and Maddox had been filling her spare time. She hadn't had time for Facebook. "I'll keep an eye out for them. Can't wait to see what you post."

She took her first right, stopping for an elderly lady crossing the street where she shouldn't be, when Dad asked, "What's in the plans for tonight? Are you working?"

"Not tonight, no. I've just finished a couple of night shifts."

"Brutal," Dad commented.

"Very," she agreed, tapping her fingers impatiently against the steering wheel, watching for the lady to inch her way across the road with her walker. "Luckily, I have tomorrow and Friday off, then I'm back to work on Saturday morning and then off again on Sunday and Monday before going into a long stretch of shifts." She lifted her foot off the brake and pressed the gas, slowly getting back up to speed once more.

"It won't always be like this, Jossie," Dad said softly. "You need to put in your time, and then you'll get the good steady shifts."

"Oh, it's not so bad," Joss said, mainly because her life wasn't all that bad right now. Sure, the hours sucked and switching from day shifts to night shifts was hell. But she had a lot to look forward to, including some filthy, dirty sex with Maddox in a few minutes.

As if Mom had read her mind, she asked, "Nothing else new or exciting?" Which in Motherland meant, *are you dating?*

Joss considered telling them that she was seeing someone, so they didn't think she was a hermit, but they'd never understand if she said that she and Maddox weren't serious. Answering endless questions wasn't in Joss's plans for the night. "Nope, same old, same old." And to get the subject shifted quickly, she added, "On Friday, I'm going to Jeremy Walsh's retirement party."

Dad piped up then. "It's about damn time he's getting outta there. Say hello to the old guy for me."

"I'll be sure to send Mr. Walsh your regards," Joss said with a smile, slowing down as the car in front of her turned right. "But maybe I'll leave off the 'old guy' part."

"Don't you dare," Dad said with a laugh.

When he stopped, Mom added in her sweet, soothing voice, "Okay, my darling, we'll let you get back to things. We're thinking we'll be coming back in few weeks' time."

"Send me flight details when you have them, so I know when to pick you up from the airport."

"Will do," Dad said.

"Love you, Jossie," Mom said.

"Love you, too. Bye."

Joss stopped at the red light and pressed the button on her steering wheel, ending the conversation. The radio came back to life. She continued tapping her fingers against the steering wheel to the beat of the music, her mind going to Maddox. She hadn't seen him since Sunday night—two whole days of hungering for his touch. Even their schedules didn't cross over, and she never saw him at the station, not a single time.

By Tuesday night, when she hadn't even gotten a text from him, she'd thought their fling had run its course, but when she'd returned home this morning, she'd found another gift box waiting for her on her front porch, along with a note giving the time she was meant to arrive at his house.

Now, the lingerie he'd bought her was on beneath her dress as she drove to his house, rested, ready, and eager.

What did he plan for tonight? More wax? More rope?

A loud honk startled her, and she snapped her eyes up to the rear-view mirror, seeing someone flipping her off. She stepped on the gas, finding, at some point, the light had turned green.

For the rest of the drive to Maddox's, she forced herself not to the think about the sexy night ahead or the slow heat building between her thighs. Only when she pulled into his driveway did she allow her mind to return to him. Her fishnet stockings felt tight around her thighs, and the garter clips still felt attached, but she almost wished she could look herself over before seeing him again, make sure everything was perfectly in place.

She exited her car and shut the door, and then her heels clicked against the driveway as she approached his red brick, two-story house. Before she could even get there, the door opened, and her mouth went dry.

Maddox filled the doorway in a dark pair of blue jeans and nothing else. No shoes, no socks, no shirt... *I am one lucky girl.*

Ripple after ripple, his body exuded masculinity. Her fingers twitched to explore him, to admire the body he clearly spent time maintaining. "Hi," she said when she reached him.

"Hi."

The slight curve to his mouth was worthy of salivation. He stepped back from the doorway, letting her enter. He shut the door behind her, then turned to her, folding his arms. "Ready to play?" he asked.

"Yes, sir." She grinned.

He looked her over from head-to-toe, then arched that left eyebrow. "You have far too many clothes on, and I'd sure like to see the gift I delivered to you today."

Slowly and playfully, she removed her dress until it fluttered to the floor, leaving her in the black, lacy lingerie.

He stayed where he was, those intense eyes watching her very carefully. "The bra, too, please."

Her belly quivered with butterflies, and a hot shiver slid through her at the power his stare contained. She reached back, unhooking her bra and letting the girls free.

When her arms lowered to her sides, he approached, glancing at her taut nipples with that sexy smile before looking her in the eye. He took her chin in his strong grip. "I want you to know that it's taking all of my strength not to fuck you right here, right now. You've not been far from my mind these past couple of days. This view…" He glanced her over from head-to-toe once more before his heated eyes lifted to hers again. "I've missed it."

She inhaled sharply. "I'm sure the lingerie helps. Thank you for the gift. It's beautiful."

His eyes narrowed. "Believe me, it's the woman in the lingerie that makes this view so stunning."

She might have thought a little bit about what that statement meant if he hadn't sealed his mouth over hers. Good God, the man could kiss. His hands slid across her face, his thick, hard body pressed against her, his tongue dove perfectly into her mouth, tangling with hers.

Only when she became breathless and rubbed herself against his erection did he break the kiss with a grin. "Impatient tonight, hmm?"

"Very," she admitted.

"Not yet," he murmured, taking her hand. "I have a surprise for you."

He led her into his living room on the right, and the moment he stepped aside, letting her see the room, her breath became trapped in her throat. She scanned the space from left to right, finding candles atop every hard surface. Too many candles to count, and since the curtains were drawn, the flames lit the room in a beautiful, romantic glow.

"I gotta be honest here," she said, glancing over the white taper candles, pillars, votives…amazed by what he'd done. "I've had a guy take me to dinner, buy me flowers, run me a bath even, but this…" She glanced at him, finding his expression soft and gentle, "…is the most romantic thing anyone has ever done for me."

He smiled, but that was his only answer.

Not that she'd expected him to comment on such a statement, and instantly, she reprimanded herself. That was emotional talk. She couldn't go there. He didn't want her to, and she didn't want to either.

She pressed her lips tightly together and watched him as he moved to the stereo next to the fireplace. There, he turned on the power, blasting electronic music through the living room.

When he turned to her again, she found intensity in him that she'd never seen before, and somehow, the music matched his mood. Sure, he could've picked something sensual, but that didn't seem to fix Maddox. The hard beats and rhythmic drums and deep bass sent goose bumps crawling over her flesh.

Though maybe it was simply the change in him causing that. Because now she saw something different there—something freer, more raw, more powerful. She saw *him,* without shields or concerns over her, and she felt something release within.

His strength, his care, his affection, she melted into it all.

He took a step forward and caught her chin in his grip. "What do you want tonight, Joss?"

"You."

—∞—

SOMETHING HAD CHANGED in her. Maddox could feel it right down to his bones, and he sensed his reaction to the way she looked at him now, the softening of the barriers he kept up. Joss stood there, bared and available, a beauty waiting for him to do any filthy, dirty thing he wanted. There in her eyes, he saw the sweet and tender moment when she'd surrendered her body to him. That trust she'd hand-delivered him warmed something dead and cold within.

Locked into her request, he held out his hand to her, and she tangled her fingers with his. He led her to the table where he'd set out the tray of toys. "Any objections to what I've decided for you tonight?" he asked, glancing down at her next to him.

Her long hair slid along her shoulder when she glanced at the black leather flogger and the red-and-black leather cuffs before she shook her head at him. "No objections."

He narrowed his eyes at her. "What was that?"

"No objections, sir." She gave a sweet smile.

He grinned and winked. "Very nice." Drawn into her smile, he brushed his knuckles across her cheeks, enjoying the way her eyes lit up when he touched her—so full of life. Determined to let the games begin, he grabbed the hair elastic and hairbrush off the antique tray and then moved in behind her. "To your knees, sweetheart."

She faced the fireplace and slowly slid to her knees. He got right to work, moving in behind her and placing the elastic between his lips as he began to brush her hair. She inhaled and exhaled with slow breaths, hands resting on her thighs. When he could easily run his fingers through her tresses, and all the knots were out, he began French braiding.

When he reached the end of Joss's hair, he fastened the elastic then tucked the braid over her shoulder. He liked the little shiver she gave him as he dragged his fingers along the long line of her neck, and his dick throbbed in agreement. The heat between them couldn't be ignored.

Ready to get started, he returned to her front, and she ran her hand down the braid, making him smile. "Surprised I can do such a thing?"

"Yes," she said with a laugh. "Very."

He'd learned the skill from spending so much time with Grey's sister, Riley, over the years. She'd always begged him to paint her nails and do all types of girly things. Something he'd never been able to refuse her. But now he only thought of one woman as he dragged his thumb across Joss's bottom lip, realizing how much he liked surprising her. Most of all, he liked seeing her smile.

With those gorgeous, heated eyes of hers on him, she sucked the tip of his thumb into her mouth before he released her, moving back to the tray again. He reached for the dark red-and-black cuffs with the soft inner lining. "Tonight, I'd prefer silence," he told her, stroking the softness of the skin on her inner arms then placing one cuff around her wrist and fastening the buckle. "The only words I want to hear from that pretty little mouth are 'Yes, sir' or our established safeword if something feels wrong. Clear?"

"Yes, sir."

Using gentle fingers and slow movements, drawing the moment out, he attached the other cuff, nice and tight, and then slid his fingers into the O-rings. "Come up now." While she rose, he examined her nipples, finding them taut. He doubted that was due to coldness in the room and assumed he'd find her cunt drenched.

Most women didn't become aroused by the anticipation of being taken, and he was only too glad that Joss reveled in these quiet, intimate moments as he did. While he kept his fingers tucked into the rings, his cock throbbed as he led her to the fireplace. Right above the mantle, he'd placed a D-ring, keeping it hidden from visitors who would never understand his sexual preferences.

While he clipped both of her wrists to the D-ring, she stayed perfectly silent. Even as he adjusted her arms straight above her head, keeping her face protected, she never made a single comment. He liked that about her. Most women talked when told not to. And the silence both calmed and warmed him, oddly more comfortable than any silence before.

Done with binding her, he stepped back, admiring his work. Her skin, her curves, her round bottom, all glowing with the beautiful warm hue of the candles, was a sight he'd not soon forget. He dragged his fingernails down her spine until he reached her ass, where he squeezed each cheek, warming her up.

She moaned, and he smiled, speaking only to ensure she felt safe. "I've never seen anything as beautiful as you bound like this, sugar."

Again, she moaned, and the desire within confirmed her comfort.

Pleased by her reaction to how he'd placed her, he ran his hand over her warm bottom before he reached for the flogger. He stepped in behind her and dragged the leather tails across her creamy, smooth back, showing her what he intended to treat her to tonight.

She wiggled her bottom, and he liked how willing she was, especially never having experienced a flogging before. That show of trust weaved around him, getting right down deep inside. He put a little distance between them, gazing over her glowing flesh, then he flicked the leather out gently, introducing her to the idea and the sensation. Her harsh breath spread out into the air when he slid his hand over where he'd struck, letting her know that his safe touch would always follow. Again, he took a step back, putting some space between them, then he tested her. Each flick of the leathers came a little bit harder until he saw her flinch, noticed the level at which she felt pain.

Now armed with the knowledge he needed to understand her, his canvas to paint, he found the rhythm of the music. Using a figure-eight pattern, he began flogging her, never going too hard, warming up the flesh that he liked seeing turn a pinkish hue.

As the minutes drew on and her moans deepened, he let himself become lost in the dance between them, connecting with her on levels that fulfilled him. A good flogging often felt like a massage, and he sensed her relax, could see the moment when she went into that quiet space of her mind where thoughts and worries didn't exist and even time stopped.

He let her stay there for a while, allowing her to enjoy the relief that a flogging brought, and even enjoyed the reprieve himself. Over and over again, he shifted back and forth on his heels sending the flogger out to her. *Thud…thud…thud…*the leather met her flesh, while the hypnotic music released all his tension as he danced with the flogger, setting them both free.

When her upper back and bottom had turned a pretty pink, he lowered the flogger. While he could've continued, as he enjoyed being connected to her this way, the relaxation didn't fulfill the intensity he craved to create. Before he moved on, he tucked the flogger under his arm and closed the distance between them, stroking her back. She startled and gasped, and he smiled. Apparently, she'd gone in deep. There was something very special in how easily she trusted him. Something he wanted to taste again and again.

He leaned in and placed his lips against her warm shoulder while he removed her panties. Feeling her quivering beneath his mouth, he slid his tongue from one shoulder to the other while he reached around and stroked her nipples. Both were erect in firm points. Curious now, he slid one hand down to the junction between her thighs and he groaned at what he discovered. A soaking wet pussy.

To show her how aroused she truly was, he slid his fingers across her drenched slit then gathered up her juices, circling her opening. She moaned, dropping her head back against his shoulder, and he rewarded her with a firm stroke of her engorged clit. Her body responded beautifully, instantly quivering, eager to blow.

He wasn't ready, not nearly done with her, and again, stepped back. Even with the space between them, the air felt charged, fueled with intensity. He waited, leaving her standing there to wonder what he planned to do before he sent the flogger hard onto her ass. He dragged the tails through his hand then sent it out to her again.

And again.

And again.

He never let up, he never stopped. Not until he reached that level where she'd earlier responded to pain. She moaned loudly and arched, and he heard her plea for more.

The music sped up, the strings of the violins being played faster and faster, and his flogging naturally followed along. Her skin flushed deeper now, a perfect shade of red on her bottom. The glow of the candles warmed the color of her skin. His canvas turning out far better than he'd imagined, his cock strained painfully to blow. The dance continued, his heart rate increased, his chest rose and fell with his heavy breaths. Only when he noticed her quivering legs did he stop. He stepped in behind her and cupped her neck, feeling her hammering pulse beneath his fingers. He slid his touch down her chest, delighted by the dampness of her sweaty flesh before he moved his hand around the warmth of her bottom. The heat against his palm brought urgency.

Though, again, he needed more. His soul wanted to claim her.

He knew he couldn't be gentle when he dropped the flogger onto the tray and grabbed the condom. Not with this beauty bound and hot and ready for him to own. He returned to her back and opened his jeans, letting them fall to his knees. Glancing over her glowing flesh, he sheathed himself in the condom. He grabbed the base of his cock, spread her cheeks, feeling the warmth of her bottom and entered her slick heat in one swift stroke, right to the hilt.

She gasped and rose on her tiptoes. He grabbed her waist, holding her to him, as he began pumping his hips. In and out, his hard cock thrust into her, straining to blow, and her inner walls clamped against him, wildly begging for a release. Skin slapped against skin. His pelvis slapping her warm bottom that he'd awakened over and over again until he felt her early quivers.

Her climax arrived with such intensity that it threatened to overtake him with little warning. Again, she rose on her tiptoes, her inner muscles squeezing his cock hard enough to make him cross-eyed. She went silent for a long moment before her scream of release blasted across him, drawing up his balls. And when she exploded, he slammed forward, roaring his release.

Time got away from him as he rested his head against her neck, catching his breath. Only when her soft whisper broke the silence did his senses return to him. Even then, it took him a minute to make out the words she'd whispered. "Thank you, sir."

Something changed in him then. Something in her voice sounded so very meaningful. Something that made him not want to hear those words, said in that husky tone, from anyone else.

Something that screamed *mine.*

~

ONCE JOSS COULD properly walk again, she went in search of food. Apparently, orgasms forced the body to refuel. When all she found was protein and vegetables in Maddox's fridge, she suggested going out. Of course, she'd expected his refusal, but she'd been armed and ready to win.

Twenty minutes later, she watched him slide into the booth across from her in the quiet pizzeria downtown, and she couldn't help but smile. She'd never seen anyone look quite as uncomfortable and miserable all at the same time.

"This feels like a date," Maddox grumbled, putting a voice to his unhappiness. "I'm still trying to figure out how in the hell you got me here."

She fought a laugh, passing him a menu. Perhaps some women would back down in the face of a growly man, but she'd grown up around cops. She'd been around strong personalities her entire life. "No, this isn't a date," she said, hoping to show him where her mind was at, which wasn't on relationship goals. "This is us getting the best pizza in Seattle because I'm starving and you had nothing to eat at your house." She grabbed the menu, giving it a once-over. "Besides, it can't be a date because I know it's *not* a date." She lowered the menu and looked at him, finding his intense eyes fixated on her. "You know, just because we're friends-with-benefits doesn't mean we can't still be friends and get to know each other a little bit better. Sometimes, friends have dinner together."

He snorted, not seeming overly thrilled about being here, but finally heaved a long sigh and glanced at his menu. "I'm not sure I agree with you, but somehow, you possess powers to coerce me that I have no shields against."

She grinned behind her menu, proud she'd gotten him to do the unthinkable. Dear God, going for pizza wasn't a marriage proposal. Obviously, he hadn't had many female friends over the years. Which only told her how much she didn't know about Maddox. Something she intended to change tonight.

Before she could dig a bit deeper into the complex mind of Maddox Hunt, the pretty blonde waitress came over. Her top, a little too tight, the V in her shirt, a little too low, and her skinny jeans looked painted on.

"What can I get ya?" she asked Maddox, holding onto her pen and notepad.

"Iced tea for me," Joss told the waitress loudly, watching the chick now openly ogling Maddox. She shook her head and glanced at the man of the hour, asking, "How about a medium pizza with all the toppings?"

He nodded. "A pint, too."

"Perfect," the waitress practically purred at him, gathering their menus in a way that put her cleavage far too close to Maddox's face. "I'll be back with those drinks shortly."

When the waitress leaned away, Joss frowned at her, but she noticed his eyes were on her, not on the waitress's girls. Glad for that, and as the waitress took off to fetch their orders, Joss set her focus on Maddox, intent to peel back his complicated layers. In a non-threating, non-pushy way, of course. "So," she said, lacing her fingers together on top of the table. "Tell me more about your family."

"Why?" He leaned back against the booth's shiny red cushion and folded his arms.

"Uh, because I want to know more about you?" she scoffed, shaking her head at him. "Is that really so weird or so terrible?"

He regarded her a minute, obviously deciding if he wanted to allow this to happen. Apparently, he did, since he answered, "I'm an only child and pretty much on my own. I have an uncle who lives in Vancouver. I think I saw him maybe three times growing up, and haven't seen him in the last ten years at all."

"And what about your parents?" she asked.

"There was only my father and me."

The waitress returned with their drinks then, and Joss ignored Ms. Googly Eyes, keeping the focus right where she wanted it. On Maddox. When the waitress left the table again, Joss asked, "You didn't have a mom growing up?"

"No."

She noted the tension around his eyes, even if she could tell he fought hard not to react to the question. Now, wondering if she should leave this type of questioning alone, she pulled her drink closer to her and held the straw, taking a sip of her iced tea. Once she'd swallowed the cool, sweet tea, she decided to press on. "Feel free to tell me to stuff it, but do you mind telling me what happened to her?"

Maddox took hold of his frosty beer glass, and before taking a sip, he replied, "She left when I was four and never came back." Then he downed a quarter of his beer.

Joss bristled, disbelieving of what she heard. To leave your child? How could a mother do that? There had to be more to the story. "Why did she leave? Did your parent's divorce or something?"

He regarded her again and then sighed, lowering his glass to the table. "My father never told me why."

"Really?" That made no sense. "Your father never shared with you why your mother just picked up and left and never came back?"

"We're men," was his dry explanation as he wiped the frothy beer off his lips. "We don't sit around and talk like you and I are doing now. Which only reminds me why I don't go for dinner with women, by the way."

She chuckled, not deterred. "Oh, come on, it's not so bad."

He arched that left brow at her. "Discussing the past only leads to memories of things you can't change, so why even go there?" He had a point, so she stayed silent as he continued. "Besides, my father hated her. Why would I bring her up?"

Interesting. She took a sip of her drink again, studying him. Maddox was tough and brooding, all muscles and confidence, not a hint of sadness about what had happened to him during his younger years. He also didn't pity himself or have any serious emotional scars she could see. Regardless of the childhood he'd been handed by having a shitty mother, he'd created a pretty damn good life for himself.

Though realizing that also made her conclude something else. "I guess I can see now why you hate commitment."

His left eyebrow arched again. "How is what I told you related at all to commitment?"

"Of course, it's related," she said, waiting for a couple to stride by their table before adding, "Being in a committed relationship isn't important to you because you've never seen what happens when two people choose to love each other forever."

She paused, watching his reaction to what she'd said.

His jaw muscles clenched twice, telling her the subject was a touchy one. "I take it you have seen that?" he asked.

She sighed, glad she hadn't overstepped, and circled the straw in her glass around an ice cube. "Yup, I have *those* parents. They're still grossly in love, even after twenty-eight years of marriage."

Maddox didn't respond to that, but she wondered if he would have if the pizza hadn't come at that moment. The waitress again went out of her way to get Maddox to notice her chest when she placed the pizza near him. Joss didn't mind one bit that Maddox stared down at the pizza, unmoving, even if she wondered what lay so heavily on his mind.

To keep things light, Joss rubbed her hands together. "See, this is so much better than broccoli and chicken." She reached for a piece of pizza, placing it on a plate and sliding that one to Maddox before taking a piece for herself, ready to dig in. Cheese, bread, meat, and grease… and a huge orgasm earlier—life had never been better. Even now, she noticed how her bottom still felt warm. She never would've believed that a flogging could feel so relaxing, and she didn't know if it was the orgasm alone, but she felt lit up inside.

She took a big bite of the pizza, moaning when the grease hit her lips, figuring they'd eat in silence, though Maddox surprised her.

"It didn't matter, you know."

She glanced up at him through her lashes, swallowing her pizza. His soft eyes were fixated on her face. "What didn't matter?" she asked.

"Not having a mother," he said, reaching for two more pieces of pizza and placing them onto his plate. Apparently, the one piece she'd given him wasn't sufficient. And that didn't surprise Joss. The man surely had a *large* appetite. He lifted his pizza to his mouth, and before taking a big bite said, "My father was enough."

She wasn't sure a mother's love could ever be replaced, but she wasn't going to tell Maddox that. It all began to make sense to her, though. Maddox didn't want a girlfriend because he didn't know what he was missing. He'd never had it, and he hadn't witnessed a good relationship as a child. Heck, she understood the need to protect oneself. He left women before they could leave him. She got it. "Does your dad live here in Seattle?" she asked.

"Yeah, he does."

She swallowed her bite, waiting for him to say more. When he didn't, she asked, "He didn't remarry at all?"

"No."

"Is there a reason for that?"

"Never asked him."

Ever the more curious. "Hmmm…"

Maddox paused with the pizza halfway to his lips, and the side of his mouth curved. "And what exactly does that 'hmmm' mean?"

"Oh, nothing really." She reached for her straw and took a sip of her drink before replying. "Just figuring you out is all."

"Perfect," he said, grabbing his napkin and wiping his face. "So now we can reach the point where you think you can fix whatever is wrong with me and somehow correct the fact that I don't want to be in a committed relationship."

She noted the dry tone of his voice, even the irritation in it. "Well," she said in a light voice, hoping he'd truly hear her, "from the way I see it, you're honorable, straightforward, hardworking, caring toward other's needs, and strong. I'm not exactly sure what needs fixing."

Maddox lowered his pizza and stared into her eyes intently. The seconds drew on as his brows furrowed. Her body heated, both under the powerful command of his regard and in all the things he wasn't saying out loud but she could hear anyway.

"But who am I to say," she added quickly to break the silence, realizing she was making things a little too emotional. "I'm nowhere near perfect, so I'm probably not the best judge of someone's character anyway."

He didn't reply, instead he gathered up his last piece of pizza. He ate the entire slice in silence before he grabbed his napkin, wiping his hands, looking at her again. "You're wrong, you know."

"Wrong?"

He pushed his plate away and stared at her with those stern eyes. “You’re the perfect *you*. The only you in this world. It doesn’t get more perfect than that.”

“Oh, you’d better be careful,” she said seriously, “I might start thinking you’re capable of being loving.”

He barked out a laugh then leaned away. “You’re right. You’re a terrible judge of character.”

Chapter 9

The next morning, Maddox awoke with a jolt. Fully aware that something was different, he snapped his eyes open and turned his head on the pillow. Joss lay next to him, snoring softly. The sun beamed through the window, casting a warm glow onto her bare thigh sticking out of the dark gray duvet. Apparently, after he'd taken her again last night, he'd fallen asleep.

That never happened. Women never stayed the night. Ever. He made sure of it. He stared at her, his gut twisting as he realized how many rules he was unconsciously breaking with her. She crashed through indestructible walls with very little effort, and without him even realizing she was doing it, and he didn't know how she fucking did that. Last night, he'd outright refused to go to dinner with her, and yet, somehow, she'd outsmarted him and basically dragged him there, making him feel like an idiot if he didn't follow.

Now, as she slept peacefully, her hair curtaining her face and her cheeks rosy, his mind churned. She lay there like a sleeping beauty for him to wake with a single kiss. He couldn't help but ask himself: *What is it about you?* Over and over again, he pondered the question, never getting a solid answer on why she captivated him so much.

He sighed, and that stirred her, causing her to rub her face into the pillow and open her eyes.

She blinked twice. Then, "Hi."

"Good morning," he said, voice tight. His head spun. What in the hell was going on with him? Last night he'd enjoyed going for pizza with her. He liked listening to her speak and watching her smile. Most of all, he liked waking up next to her. And that was a problem.

He turned onto his side and stared into the gorgeous depths of her soulful eyes, wondering how she possessed the powers she did. What sort of trickery was she using to get him to respond to her in the ways she wanted, without him even thinking about putting up his shields to stop her?

She slowly lifted her head off the pillow, giving him a measured look. "Is everything all right?" she asked, her eyes searching his intently.

Her hair was a mess, sticking up wildly, and somehow, she looked more beautiful than ever. "You confuse me."

She considered him carefully for a good few seconds before she laughed easily, rolling onto her back. "Is that a good thing or a bad thing?"

He wasn't laughing, far from it. "I don't know," he answered honestly, trying to find solid ground again. He wasn't supposed to enjoy her this much. He was supposed to curb his hunger for her, not fall further, wanting even more of her than she'd originally offered.

Her smile remained when she tucked her hand between her face and the pillow, eyes even twinkling. "Well, Mr. Serious, if you don't know if it's a good thing or a bad thing, then what *do* you know?"

"I know that I'm surprised I didn't ask you to leave last night." He hesitated, letting that truth sink in. He pushed the blanket farther down his torso, his skin flushing hot. "To be perfectly frank with you, I can't decide if your presence weakens me, or if you're smarter than me because you're crafty and getting me to do stuff I wouldn't normally do."

She burst out laughing and gave that sparkling smile he was growing fond of before replying. "Let's call it a little bit of both and leave it at that." She pushed against him, sending him onto his back as she climbed onto his lap. Her hair flowed around her face, her bare breasts dangling deliciously in his face, all stealing the thoughts from his mind. "You need to calm down and stop being so serious. Let's stop thinking and stay focused on what really matters."

He fisted his hands, afraid if he touched her, he wouldn't be able to stop. "What matters?"

She gave him a sexy grin and purred, "Getting each other off, of course." She lifted her hips and found his morning wood and rubbed her warm and wet folds against him. Back and forth, she slid her damp sex from the base to tip, until he awakened, growing harder for her.

The tease was enough to remove his hesitations. With a groan, he slid his hands up her back, as she sealed her mouth across his, teasing him with her perfect taste.

"I know where we stand, Maddox," she whispered against his mouth, "and I know that waking up next to you this morning doesn't mean that I get to leave my toothbrush here." She rubbed her clit against his hard shaft and moaned, hot desire filling her eyes.

When she moved away, he watched as the little vixen reached for the condom he'd left on the bedside table, along with the two already opened wrappers from the night before. Playfully and with that sexy smile of hers, she opened the foil and quickly sheathed his cock in the latex. He groaned as she slid her hand over him, but soon, that pleasure was nothing compared to when she held onto his cock like she owned him and lowered down, slowly taking him in.

He grasped her hip, stopping her, using his other hand to cup her nape. "You want to fuck me, sweetheart?" he asked her.

She fought against his grip on her hip, rose a little, then swallowed him up again, her long hair curtaining her face, trailing along her breasts. "Please," she breathed.

Lost in those eyes, he slid his hand across her face, bringing her mouth back to his, and tangled his tongue with hers. He kissed her until she was breathless, then he said, "Go on then, darlin'. Show me what you've got."

Letting her control things for now, he released her, laying his head back onto the pillow, watching her bounce atop him. She grabbed the headboard, holding onto that as she worked herself over him, taking him in deeply. He groaned when she arched her back, shoving her breasts out to him.

He took her up on her offer and massaged each breast, a perfect handful with taut nipples, great for pinching. She began moaning, so he squeezed harder and harder until she dropped forward, her breath raspy by his ear. She placed her head into his neck and shifted her hips back and forth, and his hands came to her hips. Forward and backward, she rocked against him, harder and faster, until her inner walls hugged him tightly. In the pulsating grip of his shaft, he sensed her climax. Doing what he could to help, he assisted her, shifting her even faster now. His cock slapped the inside of her channel until she was gasping with pleasure, and he was moaning against her slick heat strangling him.

"Fuck, you're tight and wet," he growled, pinching his eyes shut as her pleasure brought his higher, flexing all his muscles. He dug his fingers into her hips and continued bouncing her atop him, feeling her wet pussy get wetter by the second until her slick juices spread out between them.

"Maddox," she gasped, straightening up, her hands coming to his chest. Her back angled, chin pointed to the ceiling. She rocked her hips, back and forth, her moans growing louder and louder. "Oh fuck, oh fuck," she whimpered.

Christ, he wanted her to get there too because her tight cunt drove him to places he never wanted to return from. Damn sure that he'd never get enough of her, he gripped her thighs and gave her the leverage she needed, and rocked her hard, ignoring the burning of his muscles. Over and over again, he helped her fuck him with force and speed. He slapped her ass hard, again and again, until she no longer rocked her hips.

"Give me what I want," he ordered with a bite to his voice, latching on to her nipple and sucking it deeply into his mouth.

She froze.

He saw the early quivers, the pink flushing over her chest. He heard the hitch of her breath before her high-pitched scream blasted through the air, and he'd had all the teasing he could stand. He grabbed her in his arms, flipped her onto her belly then reentered her from behind.

Those screams never stopped as he pinned her beneath him with one hand pressing against her shoulder blades. Urgent now to finish, he pounded into her. Wet, sucking noises filled the air until those sounds got louder, and he felt her inner walls clamp against his shaft like a vise grip, forcing him to thrust harder and grunt against the burn in his muscles. Sweat slicked his skin as he shut his eyes, focusing on his pleasure as he felt hers rise.

Unadulterated screams he'd never heard from her filled his ears, and those sweet, beautiful sounds drew him toward the edge. Fire burned in his body as he roared and blanketed her back, becoming hard as steel. The sound of her losing control, the scent of their sex, her damp, lush body beneath him, all drew up his balls. When she unraveled, thrashing against him and soaking him, he exploded, bucking and jerking, holding her tightly against him while his seed blasted into the condom.

By the time his climax released him, he'd collapsed onto her sweaty back, while her convulsing cunt continued to milk him, greedily draining every drop. Breathless, he slid off her onto his back, arms resting at his sides, legs sprawled out, while she lay face-first on the mattress, catching her breath.

Sometime later, she lifted her face off the bed. She looked well fucked with flushed cheeks and a perfect, satisfied smile. "Seriously, are you even real?" she asked with a soft laugh.

He chuckled, sliding her damp hair away from his face. "What?"

"Honestly," she said, her head stuck to the mattress, apparently unable to move. "Emilia and I were joking that you were a Sex God, but I'm actually starting to think there might be some truth to that. I have *never* come so hard in my life. How in the hell do you do that?"

"I can do that because I care enough to take the time to understand how your body works," he told her seriously. "But believe me, Joss, I could ask you the same question."

"If I were real?" She laughed, and at his nod, she added, "What about me makes you wonder if I'm real?"

He paused. Then, "Everything."

Emotion rushed into her eyes before it was gone in a flash. She slid off the bed and said, "You've got half an hour to get to work, and I have a busy day of errands ahead of me. I should probably go." She fetched her clothing off the floor.

From his spot on the bed, he watched her round, sexy ass jiggle while she bent down and gathered her panties. Before, the distance was something he would've welcomed. Now, her running from him brought a sense of coldness he didn't like. "Come here," he said.

She turned to him, holding her clothes to her chest, and sat next to him on the bed. He started into her eyes, seeing that she had her emotions locked up tight. Not that he blamed her. He'd set up the rules, and he was the heartbreaker, after all. Regardless, he didn't like it and intended to fix that coldness.

He sat up and slid his hand across her cheek, sealing his mouth over hers. While he'd started off kissing her slowly and sweetly, he soon threaded his hand in her hair, deepening the kiss until he felt her heavy breathing through her nose and sensed her body leaning into him.

Only then did he lean away, finding her eyes heated once again. "Now you can go," he told her, regaining some of the control he'd just lost.

She chuckled softly and backed away. Her cheeks were flushed again, her lips puffy from his kiss. "Is it completely necessary to a) fuck me until I can't walk and b) always send me off wanting more of you?"

"Absolutely, yes." He grinned. "And I do it because a) I can and b) I want to."

—∾—

LATER THAT MORNING, Joss had been doing laundry at home when a text pinged her cell phone: *Meet me at Discovery Park at noon by the lighthouse.* Since the park was twenty minutes from the station, she assumed Maddox had something else going on this afternoon, allowing for a longer lunch. Whatever the reason, she was glad for the interruption from chores she didn't want to do anyway.

Once she tossed on a pair of jeans and a flowy, violet blouse and applied a little makeup, she drove the fifteen minutes to the park. When she reached the Visitor's Center, she parked her car next to Maddox's cherry-red Dodge Challenger with a black racing stripe on the hood before making the trek along the trail leading to the beach and the lighthouse.

By the time she reached the beach, her skin was flushed and sweaty, and she was only too glad that she'd worn her hair in a messy bun instead of putting in the curls she'd considered before leaving the house. But after this, she'd go back to chores, so why bother? That was the benefit of being with Maddox. She didn't have to always impress him like she would a boyfriend, trying to look perfect for him. She knew she'd get sex again from Maddox, and she knew he was happy with her not having to worry about these things.

The warm sun beamed down on her when she stared out at the water, and she smiled, breathing in the fresh air. Resting along the edge of Elliott Bay, the West Point Lighthouse stood proud, with the white tower and a small cottage tucked beside it. As pretty as the view was, nothing looked better than Maddox sitting on the rocks, staring out at Puget Sound. She felt the pull to go to him, the warm touch his closeness always brought. As she approached, she noticed they weren't alone here, telling her sexy times would have to wait. Though she also wouldn't put it past him to have sex with her, not giving a shit who saw them. But she did have some hard limits, and that was one of them.

When she reached the rocky edge and carefully began to step from rock to rock, she was glad for her flats. Maddox had yet to notice her, obviously lost in his thoughts, so she tapped her foot against the rock, saying, "Shouldn't you be working?"

He glanced sideways, the sun warming the color of his eyes. "I have a meeting at headquarters this afternoon so I booked it a little early." He gave his sexy half-smile. "And you don't need to worry. I looked around. There's not a cop in sight."

"Lucky us." She laughed, glancing at the water, taking in the view. Off in the distance, a sailboat glided by with a couple of people sunbathing on the deck. "I forgot how beautiful this place is. I haven't been here since I was a kid."

"My dad and I spent a lot of time here," he said, drawing her attention back to him.

She stared into his commanding eyes, realizing she'd never asked an important question about his father, but could only assume. "I'm guessing your dad is a cop?"

"He was, yeah," Maddox replied, leaning back on his hands. "John Hunt. He used to work with Eric, so you might have heard of him, though you were probably pretty little when they were beat cops together."

The name sounded familiar, and she shouldn't have been surprised. Cops bred cops. And Eric had been around a long time. "Maybe. Eric knows a lot of people."

She began to study Maddox and noted a softness about him that she hadn't seen all that much. He seemed thoughtful, gentle, even.

Before she could find out what was on his mind, he grabbed a plastic bag and held it up. "I picked us up some Thai on the way. Come, sit. We'd better dig in before it gets cold."

"Lunch?" she said with a sly smile, carefully making her way to a flat rock next to him. "Dear God, you'd better watch out, someone might think this is a date."

He snorted and offered his hand, assisting her to sit, and while she did, he added, "Like you said, O'Neil." He reached into the bag, taking out the Thai paper boxes. "It can't be a date if we both know it's not a date."

"I did say that, didn't I?" She accepted the box and the chopsticks, then grinned at him. "I'm so wise."

He chuckled. "Don't get cocky now."

"Don't you worry, I'll leave all that alpha cockiness to you." She liked the way he laughed now, the sound coming easier than she remembered. She opened the box, discovering that he'd brought her chicken Pad Thai. Even more curious, she asked, "And just how did you know that Pad Thai is my favorite?"

He didn't look at her, opening his box, revealing chicken and vegetables. "On your first day at the station, you brought your leftovers in for your lunch, so I went on the hunch that you enjoyed it."

"Wait. You saw me reheating my lunch?"

"I did." His mouth twitched.

She recalled back to that day. She thought she'd been alone. "I don't remember seeing you in the lunchroom."

"Of course, you don't," he said, scooping up some chicken with his chopsticks, giving her a knowing look. "I made sure you didn't see me."

She watched him eat and saw the little hint of a smile on his face. "You cannot say something like that and not tell me more. Were you looking at me a lot during that first week?"

He turned his head to her then, those warm eyes meeting hers again, causing butterflies to whip around her belly. "There wasn't a time you entered a room that I didn't see you."

There wasn't a time when I didn't feel you she wanted to say but stopped herself. There were rules he'd put in place to ensure things didn't get messy. And she'd agreed to them, welcomed them, even. Being with Maddox made sense if she kept things distant. Getting involved with a guy with clear commitment issues would only lead her to heartbreak. Nope, not going to happen.

No matter that she sensed the warmth from his admission spiral within, she couldn't walk through that door, not even once. And lately, whether because of the sex they had or maybe this softening of Maddox, she found that door wanting to open so damn bad.

She kept all the things she wanted to say locked down deep and gathered up some Pad Thai noodles, devouring them. Rules were important with Maddox because they created clear boundaries. She couldn't forget that.

While they ate, she reminded herself of all those things and watched a freighter off in the distance gliding through the water. She didn't mind the silence, but small talk kept them in a safe place. Determined to bring things back to where they needed to be, she glanced at Maddox, taking his lead from earlier. "You said you came here a lot with your father, what did you guys do?"

"Bike, hike, explore," he said before shoving a big piece of broccoli into his mouth.

"Sounds fun," she said.

Maddox nodded and mumbled with a full mouth, "We did a lot together, and most of the things we did were outside. My father loved the outdoors."

Weird choice of words. "He doesn't like it outside anymore?"

"No," Maddox said, swallowing his food. He reached for a bottle of water in the bag, handing her one first before opening his and taking a sip. "My father has Alzheimer's."

"Gosh, that's terrible, Maddox. I'm so sorry." She placed a hand on his forearm.

He glanced at her hand on his arm for a long moment before his eyes lifted to hers, looking even warmer than before. "Nothin' to feel sorry about. It is what it is." He took another bite of his lunch, then glanced out to the water. "Besides, he's happy and doing well at the nursing home he's been living at."

"What nursing home?"

"Seattle Springs."

She knew of the home and knew it was a nice place. "I'm guessing that means it's pretty bad if he's living there?"

Maddox nodded. "It might be worse if he was miserable, but honestly, he seems happier than he was before, far more content, in fact. Sure, he doesn't remember his old life or me for that matter—"

"He doesn't remember you?" she interjected gently, pressing a hand to her heart.

Maddox lowered his chopsticks back into the box and smiled gently, sliding his fingers down her arm. "Stop looking so sad, sugar. It's okay, really. When I visit him, we still have good talks and watch the games together. No, he's not the father I remember, but this is where life has taken us."

She stared at him, her chest feeling as if a hundred pounds pressed against it. First, Maddox had lost his mother. Then his father. "Well, I'm sorry, but I find this all very heartbreaking."

"Children being abused is heartbreaking," Maddox retorted, picking up his chopsticks again. "I had an amazing childhood with a man who gave me everything. I wanted for nothing. Every memory I have is a happy one. By the time the disease set in, I was a grown man, living my own life."

"Still," she said, not bothering with her food anymore. "It's tough to have your father suddenly have no idea who you are."

"You get used to it."

She sighed, wishing she could get through to him, even though she told herself she shouldn't let herself go there. More and more, she began to see the man behind the sizzling touches, and she liked him. Yes, Maddox could own her body, making her feel far more alive than ever before. Though this sweet, unselfish side of him was endearing. He made her want to love all over him, even if she knew how bad an idea that was.

"Just so you know," she said firmly, letting her barriers down for a moment. "No one should have to get used to the fact that a person who loves them is gone. Just because there's evil in this world, and worse things happen to other people, doesn't mean that what you've experienced wasn't difficult. You deserve to be loved, and I'm sorry that love for you hasn't always been easy."

Maddox finished his last bite and then gave her a soft smile. "That's a very sweet thought coming from a very sweet woman." He inhaled a long breath, and her breath caught in her throat when he glanced out at the water and added, "But in my world, that sweetness does not exist."

"Well, then, maybe it should."

He paused. Then, "Maybe."

Chapter 10

The next evening, after Maddox's day shift that had started with his mood shitty and ended the same way, he sat on a stool at the bar of Frisky Frikin—the wood-paneled, cozy, British pub—and downed the remainder of his pint. Desperate to wash away his continuing tense mood, he gestured at the bartender for another.

"Coming right up," the pretty blonde said, hurrying off to fetch his drink.

When he'd arrived at the pub to celebrate Jeremy Walsh's retirement after twenty-five years of serving Seattle, he found the pub full of his fellow cops, which wasn't out of the ordinary. This pub was a regular hangout for those on the force. Though, right now, he wanted to be anywhere but here. Christ, he didn't know where he wanted to be or what he wanted to do.

Yesterday, he hadn't known what drove him to text Joss, asking her to meet him for lunch. He only knew he couldn't stand *not* seeing her. Even now, a sense of loneliness he wasn't used to slid into him, making him feel needy and goddamn desperate. This wasn't him. He fucked women and left them, disposing of them before they could dispose of him. That's what made sense. That's what made him not hate the woman who'd given birth to him and then left. That's what had helped him get through his younger years, never wondering how a mother could leave her son and not look in on him again. That's what made him wake up every day and not miss her and not wonder where she was now.

To keep from spinning into a dark place he never went, he downed a big swig of his beer. The icy crawl of abandonment he had felt as a child crept back into him, and he downed another sip, washing that coldness away.

"Hi, Maddox."

He snapped his head sideways, and while he noted that it had been Emilia who addressed him, only Joss filled his vision. She wore a black lace top that fit her like a glove—showing the perfect tease of cleavage—and tight skinny jeans with tall black boots. She'd styled her hair down tonight with a little curl at the ends, and her makeup was dark, reminding him of when she'd shown up at his house that first night in the lingerie he'd bought for her.

His fingers tightened into fists, and it took all his strength not to move to her and take her into his arms, showing her how crazy she made him. Her shiny, pink lips called for him to taste her. Her sugary smell demanded that he devour her. Under his stare, her eyes began to dilate, inviting him to own her.

With the loud crowd around them, and his cock swelling in his pants, Maddox realized a truth he couldn't deny. Something had changed, not just in him, or her, but in the two of them together. He didn't know when it had happened or even how, but he could feel it running in his blood like extreme adrenaline.

The problem was, he didn't know what to do about it.

Before, he'd ended things when a woman showed any signs of attachment. But he didn't want to end things with Joss. Yesterday, he'd told her things he'd never told anyone about his father. She'd listened as if only he mattered and had extended affection to him, filling the cracks of coldness in his soul. Even now, he liked the way she looked at him, as if she saw no one else but him. He wasn't ready to end this yet, and she didn't seem to be either, and with that thought cemented in his mind, he realized he never wanted to be cured of his addiction to her.

"So, um…" said Emilia, obviously in response to Maddox's awkward silence and staredown of Joss, "…Maddox, this is my husband, Troy," she introduced.

Maddox blinked, forced himself to gain control, and looked at Troy. "Good to meet you, Troy." He offered his hand, noting Troy's height. At least six foot five, he towered over the women, and with his gelled, spiky, dark hair, he only looked taller.

"Nice meeting you, too." Troy returned the handshake then dropped Maddox's hand to pull Emilia into his side, nice and close. "Thanks for taking such good care of my girl on the job."

Emilia glanced up at her husband and smiled in a way Maddox had never seen her smile at anyone.

"My pleasure," Maddox told Troy. The bartender placed his beer in front of him, and he nodded in thanks, before adding, "I'm lucky to have her on my team."

"No truer statement has ever been said." Troy kissed the top of Emilia's head.

Maddox noted Joss glancing away and looking at her boots. Even he felt like a fourth wheel there. As he watched Troy and Emilia embrace each other and flirt, he wondered what that would be like. To grab Joss for all to see? To place that kind of statement out into the world so that everyone knew she was his?

Before he could decide, Troy released Emilia and said, "Why don't I get you girls some drinks? Beers?"

Joss snapped her head up "God, yes, please." She shoved her thumbs into her pockets and rocked from side-to-side. "I think I might want something a little stiffer, too, if you don't mind."

"Not at all," Troy said before heading off toward an open space at the bar.

Emilia glanced from Joss to Maddox to Joss again before calling out to Troy, "Here, I'll come with ya." She gave Maddox a quick grin before scurrying off.

Maddox sighed as the sounds around him seemed louder than before. The rock music playing through the speakers. The guy eating the peanuts next to them. The conversations all blending together in a loud roar. He shut his eyes and drew in a deep breath before he reopened them to glance around. Only a foot away stood the police chief, and near him was a female police officer Maddox knew was known to gossip around the office. Though when he looked back at Joss, he noted the way she nibbled her lip and swayed her hips. He didn't want her to feel alone. "This is difficult," he told her.

She sighed, her shoulders sagging with her soft laugh. "Surprisingly, yes."

Maddox stared into her eyes, feeling the strands of his control slipping away. Before he could somehow fix the awkwardness and make everything okay again, a hand was thrust into Joss's face.

"Joss, right?"

Maddox mentally cursed and turned to Grey, not shocked to find a beaming smile on his buddy's face. While Maddox had asked Grey to meet him here tonight for drinks, Grey's timing matched with Maddox's mood made him regret sending the invite.

"That's right, I'm Joss," she said, offering a sweet, polite smile while returning the handshake. "You're Greyson?"

"Greyson Crawford." He released her hand to smack Maddox on the back, his grin firmly in place. "My friends call me Grey, and I'm as close to a brother as Maddox's got."

"Oh," she said, eyes wide with surprise.

Maddox saw her lips part, desperate to ask more, but he also knew she wouldn't. Too much interest in him would give her away, and she was too smart for that. Seconds passed like minutes, and as the awkwardness only grew, he wondered how he could let this happen. Things never got awkward, not for him. He made sure of it.

Before he could try again to rectify things and correct whatever the fuck was going on between him and Joss, Emilia's voice suddenly cut through the air. "Joss, come here. We've got shots."

Joss heaved a heavy sigh, her posture relaxing even more. It became glaringly obvious that she wanted to get away from the tension between them as she gave Grey a tight smile. "Nice to see you again." Those pretty eyes shifted to Maddox and pierced into his soul as she added with a smile that had him by the balls, "Enjoy your night."

Maddox watched her walk away from him before he tore his gaze away. He'd created rules to ensure that things never became weird, to guarantee that he didn't falter in public, especially with so many cops around. But that fucking beautiful woman right there was breaking apart the very fabric of who he was, making him want things he'd never wanted before with anyone.

He had to fix this problem. And he needed to do it now.

Grey bumped into Maddox's arm, snapping him out of his thoughts, and as Grey turned to the bartender, he said, "Give me a pint of whatever you have on tap." He slid onto the stool next to Maddox and leaned in, keeping the conversation private. "Better be careful, you two will repeat history and end up in the bathroom of this pub doing things that could give you a lot of grief."

Maddox snorted and drank back two gulps of his beer. "That won't happen." Though even as he said it, he knew it was a lie. Everything had changed, and without hesitation, he'd take her in that bathroom and fuck the shit out of her in a second if she gave him that sexy look that she'd originally given him in the nightclub.

The look that had changed him as a man, making him want her in ways he'd never wanted anyone. The same look she'd given him at the barbeque. A look that was as equally sweet as it was sexy.

A look that screamed *mine.*

Maddox blinked out of his thoughts, watching as Grey gave one of his charming smiles to the pretty bartender, who smiled back at him.

Grey took a gulp of his beer then turned to Maddox with a knowing look. "So, after that little show there, I take it things have gotten a little more serious than you led me to believe?"

"It's not serious," Maddox stated, frowning down at his beer bottle. "I don't get serious, and you know that."

Grey snorted. "Rules are rules, yes, I know." He tipped his beer toward Maddox, his expression knowing. "Maybe it's about damn time you broke those rules."

Then what? What would happen after he broke the rules? He liked rules. That's why he liked the law. Things were clear, uncomplicated. He wasn't governed by emotions; he was led by logic. Now he didn't know which way to go. He felt like that lost little boy who'd sat on the front porch, wondering where his mother had gone.

He turned his head in Joss's direction, watching her down her shot, and felt the confusion roll through him before glancing at Grey again, "This has become complicated, but it's nothing that can't be fixed."

"Really?" Grey mused, giving something over Maddox's shoulder a quick look. "You're good then with how things are between you?"

"Yes."

Grey took a swig of his beer. "She's free to be with other men, then?"

"Of course. She's free to do whatever she wants, we're not a couple," Maddox bit off, ignoring the way his muscles seized.

"Well, good, I'm glad to hear that," Grey said, wiping the beer off his mouth before adding, "Or you might have a problem."

"What problem?" Maddox frowned.

Grey gestured over Maddox's shoulder with a flick of his chin. "The fact that your girl is in the arms of another man."

Maddox jerked his head to the side, and his chest tightened. His eyes narrowed on the guy sliding his hand across Joss's back in a way that sure looked like ownership to him. The man was so close to her, there was no distance between them, and Maddox couldn't stop watching. Logical or not, his fists tightened as a rage he'd never known before stormed through him.

No one touched something that belonged to him.

For a short time tonight, he'd thought he had a handle on himself and had even made himself believe that he could control whatever was going on between him and Joss. Now, he realized he was dead wrong.

When the man turned Joss toward him and wrapped her into a tender hug, Maddox's gaze snapped away, and he shut his eyes, inhaling and exhaling until the anger calmed. He shot off the stool, ignoring Grey calling out to him, and walked out the pub's door. Instead of doing what he craved to do: removing the guy's hands himself.

THE CITRUSY COLOGNE filling Joss's nostrils reminded her of some very happy times, causing her to nearly lean into Nick's warm body before she'd thought better of it. She quickly pushed against his chest, now inhaling the booze wafting off him, and hastily removed herself from his arms.

"Damn, Joss, you look"—his bright blue eyes roamed over her from head to toe before reaching her face again—"you look really great."

A compliment from Nick hadn't been on her to-do list tonight, but nonetheless, it felt nice to hear that rather than the last words he'd said to her when he dumped her. Besides, she probably looked fitter than he remembered. Police academy did that to a body. She studied the man in front of her, the one who'd once held her heart in his grip. He looked the same, with his all-American good looks, straight, white teeth, stylish, brown hair, preppy clothes, and a sparkling smile that could charm anyone. "What are you doing here?" she asked, shocked spitless that he was there.

He snorted a laugh, shoving his hands into the pockets of his blue jeans. "I came home to see the family and thought I'd meet up with some friends for drinks. Why? Is that a crime?" His grin turned a little devilish. "Are you going to arrest me?"

"No. No, of course, not." Joss attempted to smile and even laugh a little, but she failed miserably. She wished she'd seen him before he'd taken her into his arms to prepare herself for this conversation. Then maybe she wouldn't feel like she was Alice falling down the rabbit hole. "Sorry. I'm just surprised to see you."

The tension between his brows faded, his posture slowly relaxing. "I haven't been home in a while, but my mom kept hounding me, so I made a quick trip back for the weekend."

Which was only a reminder of *why* they'd broken up. Nick didn't want a blue-collar job and looked down his nose at those who did. He had his sights on something more white-collar, including building an empire in New York City on Wall Street. The decision to go to the prestigious, Ivy League Harvard to pursue a career as a stockbroker when Joss had chosen the University of Washington led to their demise. After he'd been introduced to the lavish lifestyle of the upper elite in New York City, his simple life in Seattle with Joss hadn't looked so appealing anymore.

I think we need a break was the last thing she remembered Nick saying to her. Now, over a year later, there he stood, half-drunk and ogling her. She stared at him, feeling like she didn't even know the guy in front of her anymore. Or maybe she'd changed so much in the last year she felt different around him.

"Yeah, yeah, get me a Heineken," he called out over the music and voices in the crowd to Timothy, another friend from high school, who was standing at the bar ordering drinks.

"On it," Timothy replied, turning back to the bartender, waving a twenty-dollar bill at her.

Joss snorted and rolled her eyes. It shouldn't have surprised her that Timothy had dismissed her as if she weren't even there. Timothy had disowned Joss when she and Nick broke up, going so far as to not say a word to her when he saw her on the street. But, seriously, how and why would someone be such a dick?

She didn't miss their friendship back then, and she certainly didn't now. Hell, staring into Nick's baby blue eyes now, she realized she wasn't the same person as when she'd last seen him and his get-along gang. It just so happened she liked the person she was now far more than the woman she'd been with Nick.

Stronger. Smarter. Sexier.

She lifted her chin a little higher when he finally looked at her again, giving her that warm smile she used to love so much. "My mom told me that you're a cop now. Congrats on that."

"Yeah, I am. Thanks." She forced a smile, wondering how his mom knew about her, but she also didn't doubt that the woman checked in on Joss's life through others. When the relationship ended, Nick's nosy mom had seemed more upset than Joss. But wasn't that the dream? Perfect family. Perfect love. Perfect white-picket fence.

Before she could barf on Nick's shiny, fancy shoes, he chuckled, nudging her arm, his eyes twinkling. "To be honest, Jossie, I can't even picture you in the uniform."

She nearly rolled her eyes at him now but refrained. Kicking him off his high horse wasn't worth her time. He also wasn't leaving, and this conversation would get back to his mother. She ignored his stupid remark and tried to be kind by asking, "How are things going for you in New York?"

"Honestly, it's amazing. I'm the youngest…" He began a string of conversation that Joss had trouble focusing on.

She narrowed her eyes, trying hard to listen to the words coming from his mouth. It wasn't that Nick's dreams didn't matter to her. She had madly loved this guy, or so she'd thought at the time. She was glad that things had worked out for him. But now, having had some distance from Nick, she found the whole conversation so materialistic, it bored her to death.

When Nick had finally stopped speaking, Joss smiled. "That's great. I'm happy things worked out for you." *And even happier I'm no longer yours.*

The song blasting through the speakers switched to something a bit harder, and a man began belting it out behind her, as Nick studied her. "You seem so different." He crossed his thin arms, giving her a thorough once-over as if she were his to examine. "I can't tell what it is. Is it your hair?"

"No." *It's my body. It's my soul.* "Nope, same old hair, same old me." And that old her hadn't been enough for him.

Now things were different, she guessed. She realized that for a long time, she'd thought maybe she wasn't enough. That if she'd been better or done things differently, he would've been happier with her. She mentally slapped herself upside the head. There wasn't a damn thing wrong with her.

Though, as she watched him look at her with a blank expression as if he didn't know her at all, she realized there wasn't anything wrong with him either. They were two people who'd once shared a lot in common until their lives took two different paths. She didn't hate Nick, she discovered. In fact, she found that she felt some tenderness toward him. He'd claimed her innocence, and that would always be special between them. She'd shared her teens and early twenties with him. But there was someone else who'd dominated her mind during her mid-twenties. Year twenty-four to twenty-five to be exact.

Nick's mouth began to move, but her mind was stuck elsewhere. On Maddox. He'd altered the course of her life, making her care less about Nick and more about what she needed to be happy. He'd kept his promises. He'd always been upfront with her. He'd helped her explore a new side of herself that she didn't even know. He accepted her for who she was, and didn't shame her for all the things she wasn't.

Being with him was easy and fun. Uncomplicated.

She turned, looking for the man who hadn't ripped her heart apart and tossed her away as if she didn't matter. By the bar, she found Grey staring at the pub's front door, drinking his beer and shaking his head, but she couldn't find Maddox in the crowd.

"Joss."

"Huh?" She snapped her head forward, finding Nick frowning at her.

"I asked if you're seeing anyone," he said.

"I…" *No, I'm not,* nearly escaped her mouth but that felt wrong. What she had with Maddox seemed far more intense than what she'd had with Nick, and they were together six years.

And that was confusing.

"You *what*?" Nick asked, waving her on impatiently.

"I have to go." She turned and strode away, hearing Nick call out to her. But he wasn't who mattered. Not anymore.

She scanned the crowd again, unable to see Maddox anywhere. Instead, she found Emilia and Troy standing near the pool tables by Jeremy Walsh, the man being celebrated tonight. "Where's Maddox?" she asked Emilia when she reached her.

"I don't know," Emilia said, glancing around. "I haven't seen him since we first came in here."

Being so tall, Troy easily scanned the area. "I don't see him."

Her stomach roiled, and she wasn't exactly sure why, only knowing that something was very wrong.

Emilia's fingers suddenly gripped Joss's arm. "Are you okay?" she asked.

The hairs on the back of Joss's neck stood up, coldness invading her body. "Yeah, yeah, I'm okay. I…I'll be right back," she said, and with steps that seemed to take a lifetime, she moved toward Grey at the bar.

He noticed her approaching and gave her a gentle smile when she reached him, before answering her unasked question, "He's gone."

"Maddox left?" she asked to be sure.

Grey nodded. "Yup." He grinned and winked. "Not that I don't love hanging with cops all the time, but now that Maddox has stood me up, I'll be on my way, too. Would you like me to send a message to Maddox for you?"

"Um…" The loud voices carried over her as bodies moved by her in a blur. Sure, it was easy to jump to conclusions about *why* he'd left. Deep in her heart, a little flutter wanted to believe that Maddox had decided for himself that the rules of the game needed to change. That maybe they could see where this relationship would take them. "Do you know why he left?" she asked.

"I can't say for sure," Greyson said, then took a swig of his beer before turning to face her more fully and giving her a knowing look. "But I would think that seeing you in the arms of another man might have had something to do with it."

She blinked. "Why?"

Grey arched an eyebrow at her. "Why would seeing you with another guy bother him?"

"Yes, exactly. Why?" she repeated firmly, holding her ground, wanting answers from someone who was clearly close to Maddox.

Grey took another sip of beer, watching her closely before he put his glass down on the bar and answered her. "To be honest, if I know one thing about Maddox, it's that he doesn't share well. Tonight, he had to share you with others in a way he hasn't since you two reconnected."

That didn't make any sense. "I thought he didn't date. How can you know that about him?"

"I wasn't born yesterday," Grey said, giving her a grin. "Maddox may not date, but I've had personal experience in my life with jealous boyfriends, and if the flare of nostrils wasn't an indicator that he couldn't stand seeing you with that guy, I don't know what is."

She gave him a *look* and folded her arms. "But he's not my boyfriend, so your theory doesn't add up."

Grey leaned forward, staring at her as if willing her to see something she couldn't see yet. "Maybe that's the problem." He grabbed his beer and tilted the tip of the glass toward her. "Maybe he should be."

—∾—

THE PUB'S DOOR shut behind him with a bang, and the night was darker than it'd been in a while, mostly due to the cloud cover from the rainy day. Maddox moved toward his car waiting for him in the parking lot. The air felt moist from the obvious rainfall that had happened while he was in the pub, and he wouldn't have minded some drops of rain to fall on him to cool him off. Since that didn't happen, he planned to go on a drive to clear his goddamn head.

Pull it together, Hunt.

For fuck's sake, he'd come all too close to removing that guy's hands off Joss in front of a pub full of cops. An epic fucking disaster, considering he'd get suspended in a heartbeat, and her reputation was on the line. He couldn't forget that little detail in all this. No matter what lay between them, their jobs were an issue that remained.

He tilted his head up to the sky and drew in the moist air, trying to get a handle on things. On one hand, he wanted to end this with Joss and put him out of his goddamn misery. Things between them were becoming complicated. Too complicated. At first, his hunger for her had him overlooking how professionally risky she was. Now, she was making him emotional. And that could only lead to him getting suspended, or worse.

On the other hand, the thought of letting her go and never touching her again gutted him. There was no way he could walk away now. His plan to shed his need for her had failed. He'd become a full-out junkie, and he knew something between them had to change, or he was going to fuck up in a tremendous way.

He lowered his head, sure the air was thicker and far harder to draw in, when he closed in on his car. Tight and tense, he rolled his shoulders, stretching out the muscles where the stress simmered. He reached into his pocket, taking out his car keys, and right as he pressed the button on his key fob to open the doors, a soft voice broke the silence.

"Why are you leaving?"

He planted his feet hard on the ground while he returned his keys to his pocket. Overwhelmed by the hot emotions swirling inside him, he pressed his hands against his car and shut his eyes, letting the coolness of the metal shed some of the heat from within. He didn't want to face her now. He didn't trust himself with her, not when she'd want answers.

Answers that he wasn't prepared to give her.

"Maddox."

Her soft voice brushed across him again, weaving its way through him to where no woman had ever touched before. She stood right behind him, but he didn't have to look to see that, he could *feel* her there. And it fucked with his goddamn head. He wanted her. All of her. Every fucking inch of her until she couldn't give him any more.

Everything was wrong, and yet it was also so very right.

The energy between them pulsed, and it surrounded him in a cloud so thick and heavy, he couldn't stand it any longer. He spun on his heels and closed the distance between them, hearing her squeak as he thrust his hands into her hair, sealing his lips against hers.

"Maddox," she gasped, trying to step away.

He glanced toward the pub, seeing no one at the door. "We're alone," he reassured her, then his lips were on hers, and he grunted as she met him with equal fervor. "That's right," he growled against her mouth, placing a hand on her lower back and tugging her into him. "Give me what I need."

She did, again and again, until his balls ached and dick hardened to pain.

Only when her body molded to his did he dare back away. A bad move on his part because once he set his eyes on her, the last strands of his control evaporated. She stood, a breathless mess of beauty, her lips swollen and pink from his rough kiss. He lifted his eyes to hers. "I'm a second away from losing all control."

She placed a gentle hand on his face, eyebrows drawn together. "What's wrong?"

"I don't like seeing another man touch you," he stated the truth harshly, not caring about the ramifications such a statement would deliver to her.

Her lips parted to respond, but he sealed his mouth across hers again, not letting her say a word. Whatever she said, he wouldn't like. She didn't want to be attached as much as he didn't. Everything she'd told him throughout their time together echoed in his ears, reminding him why it worked between them. They both held dangerous jobs. Neither wanted anything serious.

As he dove his tongue into her mouth, holding her face in his hands, he knew his jealousy was uncalled for. He didn't need her to tell him that he was changing the rules of the game. But he was fucking changing the rules, and there was nothing stopping it.

He moved his lips roughly against hers, not giving her a chance to think or speak or do anything but let him claim her. He ravished her with kisses until she began panting and wiggling against him. That was when he couldn't take any more. "I need to be inside you."

"Yes," she breathed.

He snapped his eyes open, pleased that no one was at the pub's front door, watching them. He wasn't thinking ramifications as he pulled her into the shadows by the back door of the pub. His cock throbbed in his pants, straining to blow and claim her.

There, in a dark corner, where he knew it'd be hard for anyone to see them, he eased her into that space. He held onto her arms, pinning them tightly to her body. She gasped, but obviously not a sound of fear or pain at being handled so roughly. She smelled of desire. She tasted of sin. She looked like his.

With fast and jerky hands, he grabbed his wallet from his back pocket and somehow managed to get the condom out, letting the rest of his wallet fall to the ground. He didn't look at her when he dropped his pants and applied the latex, nor did he lift his eyes as he yanked her skinny jeans down to her knees. His eyes met hers only when he shoved his thick cock into the small space between her thighs. She stared at him intently, desperation flooding her expression in the seconds before he shifted his hips, finding her slit, and entered her.

Some nights were for pleasure. Tonight wasn't about that, and Maddox knew it. *Mine* echoed in his soul as he pumped his hips, possessing her. Desperate to get closer, he bracketed her face and stole the moan she offered, taking each one as if even those belonged to him.

She grunted when he fisted his hands in her hair. He gritted his teeth and pounded into her, sliding his mouth to her neck where he bit the skin there. He heard the hitch of her breath and felt her hard tremble, so he bit harder and harder until she was quivering.

He wanted to mark her, every goddamn inch of her. Holding her tighter to the wall, keeping his body over hers to protect her from anyone who dared to come between them, he shifted his hips harder, sliding up into her until he couldn't push anymore. She moaned loudly, and he slapped a hand over her mouth, keeping her silent as he took what belonged to him.

In and out, his cock branded her, exactly as he intended.

Then he opened his eyes, locking gazes with hers, and the heat, the tension, the adrenaline flooding him eased. There in her eyes, he saw something he never wanted to let go of—dark pleasure. His balls drew up tightly against his body. With her, he couldn't hold back, he couldn't wait.

In his mind, this wasn't about pleasure, at least it hadn't started out like that, but the look in those eyes changed everything. Her soul had changed him. She *owned him.* And there was no going back. He pumped his hips hard and fast and growled an inhuman sound. The sudden rush of endorphins flooding him, feeling her climax rolling into her, all had him slamming his hips forward and grunting his release.

He dropped a hand to the brick wall behind her, pressing his forehead against hers, giving himself the minute he needed to recover.

"Maddox," she whispered.

When he lifted his head, her worried eyes met his, her hand coming to cup his face again. "Are you okay?"

"I'm fine," he said, leaning away, out of her reach. "You should head back inside."

"Okay, hold up," she retorted, grabbing her pants and wiggling back into them. "You go from *that* to asking me to leave with your dick still out? What in the hell is going on with you?"

"Nothing. I'm fine," he told her, and himself. "We could get caught out here. That's something neither of us wants. I'll be there in a few minutes. Promise." All lies. Nothing was fine.

"Okay, I'm going to believe what you're telling me," she said gently before rising on her tiptoes to kiss his mouth, softly, intimately.

It wasn't a kiss he was used to, and that was what made Joss so different. She held confidence with him. She didn't shy away from his strong personality. She met it head-on and never let him push her away. She melted into him as if her soul undeniably trusted him, and that's what kept him coming back for more.

He couldn't ever forget her.

When she'd broken the kiss, he reached for his pants, pulling them up over his hips. Then she said, "Don't be long, okay? Now that we've gotten that out of the way, surely we can handle one night of keeping our hands off each other."

He faked a smile because she smiled at him. She thought this was passion. She thought he couldn't control his lust around her, but she was wrong. *You are mine, sugar.* And that was the fucking problem. Not only because of their jobs and the complication that came with that. But because he didn't love women. He didn't need them. Because the second he did, it might make his mother leaving a little more real, a little more raw, a little more of something he had to face and deal with.

When she slid out from under his arm, he kept his hands pressed against the brick wall, knowing if he didn't, he'd grab her again and fuck her until she drained him dry. He dropped his head, catching his breath, hearing the clicking of her heels moving off in the distance.

Below his feet lay his wallet on the damp pavement, wide open and showing his bank and credit cards. He'd known many men who kept a photo of their women in their wallets. He'd never understood that desire before. The need to make sure someone was always with you.

Until now.

Chapter 11

When Joss had left for work this morning, the sky was bright and sunny, the wind barely there. Her mind was on Maddox and the way he'd changed last night at the pub. Something seemed different about him—conflicted for sure. She kept telling herself to stop thinking about what was on his mind and just keep enjoying the sex he gave her, leaving it at that. But her mind kept circling back to him, every damn time. She figured her day would be spent in a vicious cycle, wondering over Maddox and telling herself not to, over and over again. That was until a couple of hours into her shift when everything changed.

Hours upon hours Joss had spent learning about tragic deaths at the academy. She'd even learned how to handle tragedies with the greatest of care. Though when she arrived first on the scene of the three-car accident, her training couldn't have properly prepared her for the real thing.

The call had come in mere moments before, and Joss had only been a couple of minutes away from the accident. She put her police car into park and flicked her siren off, but left the lights still flashing. She'd parked her car sideways across the road, blocking any other cars from getting close, remembering all the training she'd been given.

While she exited her police car and moved to the scene at the T-intersection, a sense of calm descended. "Stay back," she ordered to the crowd, who had gathered on the corner of the road. "It's not safe. Stay back."

The crowd stepped back onto the sidewalk, and some even began returning to the burger joint they'd obviously come from. That's when Joss noticed all the phones pointed at the scene, filming the destruction that had happened on this beautiful sunny Saturday morning. She stayed focused on her job, ignoring the phones now pointed at her, and scanned the area.

Across the road was an abandoned gas station, with a body shop kitty-corner to the burger joint. There was no sense of danger now, but as she took in the mangled cars in front of her, she suspected that death had come calling.

Pieces of ripped apart metal were scattered from one side of the road to the other. The smell of burnt-chemical from the deployed airbags lingered heavily in the air when she approached the first car, and the scent of engine coolant from an obviously cracked radiator wrinkled her nose.

When she reached the red Honda, she heard a soft cry but couldn't distinguish exactly where it had come from. The bumper of the Honda was bashed in, and a man sat in the driver's seat. He was slumped over, blood pouring from a wound somewhere on his face. She slid her hand through the broken driver's side window, immediately catching the scent of booze wafting off him. *A drunk driver*, she thought to herself as she pressed her fingers against his pulse point. The man moaned.

"Sir." She squeezed his shoulder. When that didn't work, she dug her fingers into his arm. "Sir. Wake up."

He moaned again and mumbled something incoherent. She'd seen the same reaction many times from people who were drunk and disorderly. He looked about three-times over the limit, and he didn't seem injured past the cut on his head.

"The paramedics are a minute behind me. Stay inside your vehicle," she told him, not wanting to move him in case she was wrong about him being completely shitfaced and he had neck injuries.

Besides, there were others that needed her. She had to keep going. And his car wasn't about to go up in flames.

While she hoped that her backup and the ambulance got there soon, she forced her feet to move forward, even though she felt sick with guilt at leaving an injured man behind. The crowd behind her grew restless, and she could hear them talking amongst themselves as she closed in on the second car. The soft cry came again, but she still couldn't make out where the sound was coming from or if the person was male or female. Regardless that she wanted to find the person belonging to that cry echoing in misery, she couldn't allow her mind to stray. She kept her thoughts centered on her job.

When she reached the black Jeep, she noted that the front had been smashed in quite a bit, but she couldn't see any other damage or smell any hints of fire or gasoline. She reached the driver's side window. It must've been open at the time of the accident because she didn't find any broken glass. She peered inside, finding two young women in the car, maybe eighteen at most. "Are you both all right?" She couldn't see any visible wounds on either of them, but the airbags were deployed, and both girls looked shaken.

"Yeah, yeah, we're okay," the driver said, sudden tears welling in her eyes.

"Can you move?" Joss asked.

"I think so," the passenger said, her chin trembling.

Joss unlocked the driver's side door and then opened it, holding onto the young woman's arm as she exited. "Go sit by the tree over there." She pointed at the old gas station. "The ambulance will be here shortly." She held onto the driver a little bit longer until she felt stable on her feet.

As the driver moved to safety, Joss quickly helped the passenger across the street before moving on to the last car at the scene. Her chest clenched as she prepared herself for what she'd find. The last car was in the worst shape. Beaten up from the front and the back and the right side, Joss couldn't even tell what kind of car it was, only that it was navy blue.

The driver's door was open, but both airbags had been deployed. She leaned into the car, finding the windshield smashed in, and she imagined that meant that somewhere out in front of the car lay a body. Her throat tightened as the soft cry came again, and this time, she knew it had come from someone who'd been in this car. She drew in a deep breath, preparing herself to find death greeting her, but that's not what she found.

A man sat up with his back to her.

"Sir," she said, slowly moving toward him. "Sir. Police. Are you all right?" Upon further inspection, she noticed that he was holding onto someone, and that someone had blood covering her from head-to-toe. Obviously, she'd been the one who had gone through the windshield. "Sir. Police."

"My wife," the man said, his voice soft and distant. "She took her seatbelt off to reach for her bracelet on the floor. It was only for a second. She only took it off for a second..."

"Sir," Joss said again, placing her hand on his shoulder, and he turned his head, meeting her gaze.

In that moment, all her training failed her. Nothing could have prepared her for dealing with someone else's emotions when the pain was this raw, this real, this soon. She fought tears, her lungs fighting for air. "Sir," she managed. "Please let me see if I can help her."

He shook his head, tears spilling from his eyes. "There's nothing you can do for my Rosie. She's gone."

Joss swallowed emotion and went to her knees next to him, reaching for the woman wearing the pretty, flowered dress covered by splatters of red.

"No." The man squeezed his arms tighter, pressing the side of his face against his wife's, regardless of the blood between them. "No, don't take her. Not yet."

"I won't take her. I promise." She moved in slowly, pressing her finger against the woman's bloody neck and shut her eyes, wishing for a *thump* indicating that this woman's life wasn't over yet.

Her wish never came true.

Blaring sirens erupted and snapped Joss into action. She placed her hand on the man's shoulder again and said the only thing she could think of. "I'm so very sorry." *So very sorry I can't bring her back to you.* Her legs were shaky when she rose and glanced over the mangled car, discovering two other police cars were on the scene now, plus a fire truck and an ambulance.

At Joss's feet, the man sobbed, rocking his wife. "My Rosie. My poor, lovely Rosie."

"What have you got?"

It took Joss a second to realize a paramedic was talking to her. She turned her head and shook it.

"DOA?" the paramedic mouthed.

Joss nodded.

No emotions had shown on his face before he hurried off toward the girls at the gas station. That was the job, and Joss realized she needed to learn that skill of keeping emotions out of it as she glanced at the man at her feet again.

When his sad eyes met hers, she could barely breathe, and tears prickled her eyes when he whispered, "She was my everything."

LATER THAT NIGHT, Maddox arrived at Joss's a little bit before dinner, finding her car in the driveway. He'd had today off, and spent the morning at the gym and then the rest of the afternoon servicing his car. Until the call from the sergeant in his division updating him on the accident brought him to Joss's doorstep. Dealing with any kind of trauma was an adjustment for new rookies, and even Maddox still remembered the worst ones he'd seen in vivid detail. Those horrors never went away.

While last night weighed heavily on his mind, as did the fact that he'd lost control of himself, he needed to see her. Once he reached her front door, he knocked and waited, but she never came. He considered leaving, but his instincts told him not to. She shouldn't be alone after what she'd seen today. In fact, after a hard scene, Maddox always spent time with Grey because Grey didn't see the things Maddox did, and somehow, his friend always grounded him. That was his way to unload and get his head right after seeing things that no one should ever see.

He reached for the door handle, finding the portal unlocked, and as he opened it, he called, "Joss?"

"In here."

The coldness in her voice strained the muscles across his shoulders, causing him to hurry inside and shut the door behind him. Only a few steps down her hallway, he found her sitting on the couch in her living room. Her legs were tucked underneath her, a blanket wrapped tightly around her, and a glass of red wine was in her hand. "I heard about today," he told her, noting her puffy eyes and pink cheeks. Obviously, she'd been crying.

"You did?" she whispered.

He nodded and approached her, hastily taking the wineglass from her hand. "This isn't a good idea." He placed the glass behind him on the coffee table out of her reach before turning to her again. "Never drink after a bad scene. It won't lead anywhere good. Talk about it to those who understand the reality of seeing the things we do, but don't wash away what you feel with booze."

She stayed silent, staring deeply into his eyes.

He frowned at what he saw in her expression. She'd always been such a bright light. Strong and steady. Not now. She was entirely something different. Something dark. "Talk to me," he said gently.

She paused. Then, "I'm not okay."

"I see that." Right then, he realized that when she wasn't okay, he wasn't either. A heavy feeling sat in the center of his chest. He needed to touch her, not only to be close to her, but for himself. The distance between them gutted him. He took a step forward, but her sharp voice stopped him.

"Please don't come any closer."

A chill ran through him, and he became instantly alarmed at the emotion in her voice and her eyes. "Please tell me what you're thinking," was all he could think to say.

She pulled the blanket up to her chin, staring at the wineglass in front of her on the table. "I imagine you came here because you think the death today rattled me."

He shoved his hands into his pockets, fisting his hands. "Hasn't it?"

"A little, of course, but it's not the woman's death that I can't stop thinking about."

The coldness in her voice tightened his jaw. She didn't sound like herself, and he didn't realize how fond he'd grown of the warmth she exuded until it was gone. "Then what's upset you?"

"The husband," she replied, still staring at her wineglass.

"The man you saved?" he asked, not understanding.

She nodded, eyes glossing over, obviously lost in a memory. "When I arrived and found him, he was holding his dead wife in his arms." She shut her eyes, closing out the world, a haunted look crossing her face. "When I moved to him, he told me that she was already gone and there was nothing I could do to help her."

"You can't control whether someone lives or dies," Maddox added gently, hoping to pull her out of the darkness. "I'm sure you did what you could to help them."

"I'm not upset that I couldn't help them." Her eyes stayed shut, but a single tear slid down her cheek. "What upsets me is what he said to me."

Maddox stared at the tear that slowly but surely gutted him, a coldness sliding alongside the blood in his veins. "What did he say?"

"'She was my everything.'" She paused. Then she opened her eyes, and emotion hit Maddox straight in the chest as she added, "But it was how he said it. The connection I had to him in those seconds where he realized that his happy life as he knew it had ended."

Maddox's throat tightened, and he folded his arms, fighting against himself not to move to her and take her into his arms. She might have told him to stay away, but all he wanted to do was go to her.

She drew in a long, deep breath before speaking again. "A stranger that I don't know changed me today." Her green eyes held his blue gaze, so much being said without saying anything at all. "And as I've sat here since I came home, I can't help but wonder what we're doing."

His lips parted to answer her, but his reply never came. It would have been easy to say that maybe, just maybe, he could try a relationship with her and see how it worked out, but she was right. It was one complication after another with them. A relationship with her was never in the cards. Their jobs were a hefty barrier between them and couldn't be ignored.

She sighed at his silence and slowly shook her head. "I mean, we're not dating, but kinda-sorta dating. We're not committed to each other, but you're not okay with another guy getting close to me. I know this was all supposed to be fun, but *is* it only fun, or are we fooling ourselves?"

Beneath his folded arms, his fists clenched, his chest rising and falling quickly with his heavy breaths while she continued. "Tomorrow, you'll still be my superior, and I'll still be your subordinate. You could get suspended for starting a relationship with me, and that's drama I don't need at the beginning of my career." Her eyes glazed over; obviously, her thoughts running rampant. "Nothing will change these truths. Nothing we can do will change the outcome of what's standing in our way."

I want to keep you was what he wanted to say. Again, words failed him. Not because he couldn't say them but because it was unfair of him to put her in that situation. *Just sex* made sense. Anything more would complicate everything. Those were truths he couldn't ignore.

As if reading his mind, she added, "Before, I guess you were right when you said I was the kind of girl who wants love. Maybe I forgot. Maybe it's because I'd been hurt before, I don't know. But I am that girl, and nothing I do will change that." She hesitated and sighed deeply before she went on. "I don't know when things got so messy or complicated, but they have, haven't they? And pretending they haven't is only going to take us down a road that can't lead anywhere good."

He glanced at the floor and shut his eyes, wanting to rewind time to before he'd touched her. Because she was leaving him. He knew it, and the life slowly began to squeeze out of him, seemingly all too familiar.

Obviously unable to see the torture within him, she added, "Just because I didn't find the kind of love I saw today with Nick, and I can't have that with you, it will never change the fact that I *want* a man to look at me that way. I *want* to be his everything."

Maddox could barely breathe, but he managed, "I never wanted to hurt you."

"I know you didn't, and as of right now, you haven't." She gave him the softest, sweetest smile. "But we've changed, haven't we? This is no longer *just sex.* Somewhere along the way, we complicated things. I know you care about me. I don't even question that. But can you ever do what a man needs to do to love a woman? To pick her over everyone else? To stop having her be a secret and make a statement to the world that she belongs to him? To stop thinking she's like your mother and going to leave you? I honestly don't know."

Her last words were like a knife to his gut, and he locked his knees not to wobble when she continued. "I like you, a lot, in fact. But I promised myself I'd never make things this complicated again. Us… *this*…it wasn't supposed to be like this. We were supposed to have sex. But now, everything is different. And I can't hope and wonder if you're going to be the guy I need you to be because then I'm setting myself up to get hurt." She paused. Then, her voice and expression hardened. "I won't do that again. I want a guy who wants me back. Fully and completely. Not in a way that suits him." She blinked, and when her eyes locked on to his again, he realized he'd already lost her as she said, "I promised myself I would never be that quiet girl who sits back with a perfect smile, pretending that everything is okay. Not again. I need something real. I need something honest. And we had that for a little while."

His breath caught in his throat as she rose from her spot on the couch. With each step she took toward him, the air seemed impossible to breathe. A soft smile reached her face as her hands came to his forearms, and he felt his muscles strain, though not from the heat of desire. This was a desire to grab on to what belonged to him and keep her safe.

"I'm sorry that this got complicated. I never wanted that. You've been nothing but amazing to me, and I don't regret a single moment with you." She hesitated then, and that's when Maddox saw what this was truly all about. She cared for him, deeply, it seemed, and this was self-preservation. "But right now, I can walk away from you without hurting. If I let this go on any longer, I won't be able to do that."

His heart hammered in his ears as she stood on her tiptoes and pressed her warm lips against his in a sweet, soft kiss that said so much without saying anything at all.

When she backed away, tears slid down her cheeks. "Goodbye, Maddox."

The room closed in on him, a cold sweat washing over him as she strode away. Then the world as he knew it spun on its axis as her bedroom door clicked shut.

Chapter 12

The following night after the breakup, and unable to sleep or get anything right in his mind, Maddox left his house for the gym but instead arrived at Seattle Springs, the nursing home where his father had lived for two years. Everything looked different now, nothing the same. Truth was, he didn't know how to fix everything, but he didn't know how to let Joss go either. He strode through the main doors and turned right, entering the sitting room.

He leaned against the doorframe and smiled, staring at the man sitting in the corner by the window, reading a book. Amusing to say the least because, before Alzheimer's, his father had hated reading. That was the weirdness of the disease. His father didn't even act like himself anymore, except for being a night owl. Once a stoic, hard-ass cop, now he'd become a scholar who discussed things that forced Maddox to read a few books so he understood what his father talked about.

"Today's a good day."

Maddox turned toward the sweet voice, finding Nancy, a nurse that'd been at the nursing home since his father moved in. "Those have been few and far between. Any reason for the change?" Maddox asked.

Nancy half shrugged, giving her gentle smile. "I'm not sure, but he's been like this all day. He's very lucid and aware. Go talk to him while it lasts." She turned on her heels, picking up a tray with plastic drinking cups on her way out into the hall.

Maddox moved toward the two cotton wingback chairs resting in front of the bay window. "Hello," he said with a smile, not using a name since that could set his father off. He'd been everything from George to Harry to Edward, but never John, his real name. "I'm Maddox, and I'd like to visit with you today if that's all right." Which is what the support staff told him to say whenever he approached his father.

"Yes, of course, please take a seat," said John, closing the book and putting it on the round side table next to him.

Maddox took his seat, finding his father dressed in a white shirt with a blue sweater overtop and beige slacks. Appearance-wise, no one would ever know there was anything wrong with him. He had the same bright eyes, the same color as Maddox's. Same medium build. Same deep wrinkles around his eyes. Same gray hair. But this man was a shell of what his father used to be. "What book are you reading there?" Maddox asked.

"It's a love story I found on my bedside table this afternoon after my nap, along with a whole basket of things," John said sheepishly. "I know it seems silly for a man of my age to read such things, but I was such a failure at love during my life, I wondered how other men managed it."

Maddox smiled, not commenting on the fact that his father before would've bet a million dollars he'd never read a romance novel. The truth was, his father probably made up a whirlwind romance in his mind that didn't even exist. "You couldn't have been that bad with the ladies, a handsome fella like yourself."

John barked a laugh and slapped his once strong leg that now looked far frailer. "I did enjoy my fair share of ladies, of course, but there was one woman who mattered above all the others."

Nancy returned then, placing two hot apple ciders, a new favorite drink of his father's, onto the coffee table between them. "Thank you," Maddox said to her before picking up the mug and addressing his father again, indulging the conversation. "Tell me more about this woman."

He took a sip of his cider, as his father explained, "She was the mother of my only son."

"You had a son?" Maddox asked, lowering his mug back to the table. Last time, his father had said he had a daughter, which of course wasn't true. The time before that, he'd had twins.

John began to frown. "No…no, I don't know why I said that."

"About this woman," Maddox added quickly, moving the conversation along not to let John get too focused on what he didn't know. The key to pleasant conversations with John was not reminding him of all the things he couldn't remember. "Was she pretty?"

"Pretty?" John said, a big smile spreading across his face, eyes twinkling. "She was one of those girls that shined as bright as a million suns in the sky."

Maddox chuckled. Apparently, the old man had been reading quite a few romance novels.

A thought he kept to himself as John continued. "For some reason, she married a guy like me"—a sudden darkness rose to his face, voice growing thicker—"and, truthfully, that was the biggest mistake she could've made. I was her demise."

Maddox leaned forward, resting his elbows on his knees. "What do you mean by 'her demise?'"

John sipped his cider before putting his mug back on the coffee table. "I never told her I loved her, can you believe such a thing?"

"Yes, actually, I can," Maddox said, never having said those three words to any woman either. It was not something built into his vocabulary. He couldn't recall his father having ever said it to him either.

"I'm not sure why that seemed so hard at the time, but it was. It felt like it weakened me to say it, or maybe it gave her control over me. I'm not sure. It's something I've wondered over the years, you know. Was it because no one ever told me 'I love you?' Could it be that I never learned from my parents how to express emotions like that?"

Maddox reached for his cider again, washing away the discomfort rising in his throat. "What happened to this woman?"

"She died."

There was a ring of truth to his father's voice, a little more clarity than usual. As odd as it was, there was something inside Maddox, telling him to dig a little here when normally he wouldn't. "When did she die?"

Another orderly walked by, heading down the hallway when John answered, "A week after she'd left my son and me. She'd been in a car accident, and I was called because I was her next of kin."

Maddox frowned. "You can't think you're responsible for her death."

"It's my biggest regret in my life," his father added dryly, reaching for his mug and taking another sip. "If I'd only treated her better, she wouldn't have left us. She wouldn't have been driving that night to look for a new apartment suitable to raise a child."

Maddox almost commented on the child again but knew to stay away. This was the most his father had talked in at least six months. Usually, his conversations were so far out there, it was hard to follow along sometimes.

Letting his father go on, Maddox stayed silent, as John said, "If I'd called her and begged for her to come back… If I had worked less and been there for her more. If I had treated her like the angel she was. She'd still be here, not only for me. But also for my son." He suddenly reached into his back pocket and pulled out his wallet, then he took out a black-and-white photo, offering it to Maddox. "This is my Lilianna."

At his mother's name, Maddox froze, unable to speak, and squeezed his fingers around the picture of his mom and him. He tried to get his mind around this, reading between the lines to gauge if this was another of his father's stories. Back when he was a young kid and had asked why he didn't have a mom, his father replied, *"Because some kids don't. Sorry, buddy, I'm all you've got."*

He'd never asked again. Even as a young boy, he'd seen the discomfort his dad felt at having to have that conversation. It was never said but fully understood. Now, as he looked at his mother's sweet smile and long, flowing, golden locks, he wondered if he should've asked more. And fought for the answers he hadn't known he wanted until this moment.

Those thoughts led him down a path of wondering if the anger he'd felt toward women growing up might have only been anger at himself for pushing them away. Before he could spiral out of control, and knowing the likelihood that this story could also be completely made-up, he asked, "Did you tell your son about what happened to his mother?"

"No." John hung his head, voice soft. "No, I'm afraid I didn't."

"Why not?"

"Because I was so deeply ashamed," John said softly, placing his mug back onto the table and linking his hands together on his lap. "I know what you must think of me, but I was so embarrassed that my failures had led to his mother leaving. That she felt a new life was better than the life she had with me. Then I couldn't face telling him the truth. That I had caused her death."

Maddox's chest rose and fell with his heavy breaths. He couldn't be sure his father was even telling the truth, but a little voice inside believed him. And he didn't know what to do with this information.

John ran a hand over his face and drew in a long, deep breath before speaking again. "Do you think if I had told my son the truth, he would've forgiven me?"

Maddox stared at a stranger. So honest. So transparent. So regretful. So emotional. So unlike his father. Above all else, he stared at a man who'd done his best for him, and Maddox had only good memories. "Yes, I do think if you had told your son the truth, he would have forgiven you." He paused. Then, not only for his father but for himself, too, he added, "And I'd bet he never would have blamed you at all."

One second, John gave a soft, warm smile. The next, his expression became a little colder, a bit detached. "What were we talking about?" He blinked, his eyes widening, fear present in their depths. "Who are you?"

Maddox rose, taking his exit before an outburst happened. "Sorry to disturb you, sir. I'd brought you a cup of cider." He pointed to the half-drunk mug on the table. "I thought you might like a drink before bed."

"Ah, yes, yes I do. Thank you." John picked up the warm beverage and glanced out the window, taking a long sip as if he hadn't dropped the biggest bombshell on Maddox's life. As Maddox turned to leave, John piped up. "Oh, and if you don't mind, please tell that nurse Joss to come back. She was so lovely."

"Sorry," Maddox said slowly. "Did you say *Joss*?"

"I believe that was her name," John said with a smile. "She came to see me today. I think…or was that yesterday?" He paused, shaking his head, then added, "I wonder if it was her who brought me this book."

"This nurse," Maddox pressed, still reeling, "what else did she bring you?"

John pointed over Maddox's shoulder. "Have a look. It's all right there."

Maddox moved toward the basket sitting on a table. His dead, cold heart skipped a couple of beats as he stared at what was obviously a care basket. Countless books in different genres. Candies and mixed nuts. "Did she say why she was here?" he asked.

Nancy entered the room and answered with a gentle smile, "To visit a fellow cop who deserved some company."

Knowing Joss had been sweet and thoughtful had never been a question in his mind. He glanced back to the gift basket and realized that sweetness made her unforgettable by not only him but also his father, a man who couldn't even remember his son.

—

TWO DAYS AFTER the breakup, and early into the morning, Maddox had slept only a handful of hours. The sun beamed through the window, and from his place on his couch, Maddox glanced up from the coffee table to find Grey entering the living room, as was the norm every Sunday morning.

"What's all this?" Grey asked, waving to the pile of papers spread out on the table. "And why are you not ready for the gym?"

Working out was the last thing on Maddox's mind. He leaned back on his couch and folded his arms. "Documents about my mother."

Grey's brows shot up to his hairline, and as he settled into Maddox's favorite black leather recliner angled perfectly toward the TV in the corner of the room, he asked, "What documents?"

Maddox was sure he'd spoken to Grey about his mother over the years, but it wasn't often, which explained the curiosity shining in Grey's expression.

"Yesterday I went and visited my father," Maddox explained, staring down at the photograph of his mother. He discovered he looked a lot like her. Same hair color, same eyes even, only she was far more feminine than him with soft features. "Of course, my father didn't know it was me," Maddox added to Grey, "but he began telling me a story about the love of his life and how he'd wronged her enough that she left him."

Grey glanced over the documents on the table with a frown before looking up at Maddox again. "That's not what he told you before, right?"

Maddox shook his head, ran his hands over his face, and drew in a deep breath before answering, "I can only recall him ever talking about her once. I think I was six, maybe, and had asked about her. He told me that she'd left us. He never explained to me why, or why she hadn't come back."

"Did he tell you why she left when you saw him yesterday?" Grey asked.

Maddox picked up the driver's license photo of his mother that he'd gotten from the DMV. Lilianna Hunt was a beautiful woman but appeared haunted, troubled. Even now, Maddox swore he could see the pain of her life in her face, especially her eyes. He stared into them now, as he began explaining what his father had told him yesterday.

By the time he was finished, Grey's mouth was set in a firm line. "I suppose that gives a reason for *why* she left," he offered.

Maddox nodded. "It does." And while that fulfilled the little question inside him—*how does a mother leave her child?*—the part of his soul where a mother's love should be, remained cold. "But it's the reason she never came back that's far more interesting."

"What reason is that?" Grey asked.

Maddox picked up the police report in front of him that he'd printed off, offering it to Grey.

Grey's eyes scanned over the document then his gaze returned to Maddox in a flash. "Fuck, man. She died?"

Maddox bobbed his head, wishing that hadn't been the case. There'd been many times over the years that he nearly considered looking into her. He had the means to at the station, but he'd always stopped himself, thinking she wanted nothing to do with him. "Honestly, I didn't think the old man was telling the truth when he told me yesterday." Because he didn't think his father would ever lie to him. Their relationship had been good, tight. His father had been there for every football and baseball game. An honorable, good cop, Maddox had been proud to be his son. This didn't make him proud. "From what I've seen, it appears he was right—she died a week after she left, while she was out looking for an apartment to raise me."

Grey read the report detailing the accident again and then shook his head in obvious disbelief. "I don't understand why your father would keep this from you."

"Shame," Maddox offered the only thing he could come up with. And he'd considered every option out there. "From what he said, he felt responsible for her death. I can only imagine that he didn't want to upset me."

"Or he didn't want to face the truth himself." Grey tossed the paper back onto the coffee table. "I guess that explains why you look so torn up. Have you even slept?"

"Not much." Maddox dropped his head and ran his hands through his hair, trying to get ahead of this. "I wondered from time to time why she never came back or even checked in on me." He lifted his head, looking at the one person who'd always been a constant in his life. "I couldn't wrap my head around what kind of mother would do that?"

"A terrible one," Grey muttered.

"Exactly, but was she so terrible?" Maddox rubbed the back of his neck, trying to ease the tension in his muscles. "Or have I punished the wrong person my entire life?" All night long and into the early morning, he remembered all the times he'd cursed his mother when he was younger. He remembered the time in his teens when he'd decided he didn't need her or any woman for that matter. And he vividly recalled the time he'd decided not to live in the pursuit of love but put his career above his personal life. Though without his mother as the enemy, those choices would have never been made. "Fuck, I don't even know why I'm thinking about all this shit. It's in the past. It's done."

"Oh, I know why you're up in arms," said Grey, leaning back in his seat, resting his ankle on his opposite knee. "It's because when you start questioning yourself about your mother, you start wondering why you haven't made the sweet lady in your life a little more permanent."

"This isn't about Joss, it's about my mom," Maddox bit off, rising to his feet. He moved to the window, staring out into the cloudy day.

"Bullshit," Grey countered. "Why do you think I've been razzing you?"

Maddox snorted, not looking back at his friend. "Because you enjoy irritating me."

"Well, yeah, I do," Grey said with a soft chuckle. "Regardless, I'm saying she's getting under your skin because she can, and that's never happened to you before. She's different. You're different *with* her."

Maddox snorted again, then he turned to Grey. "What are you, my therapist?"

Grey didn't even flinch, holding his stare intently. "We're as close as brothers, Maddox. I know you, and I know what this woman is doing to you, even if you don't want to accept it."

Maddox knew he'd typically shut down here, ignore what Grey had to say to him, and tell him to fuck off. Instead, today, for whatever reason, he couldn't. Everything was different, and he couldn't get a handle on anything. "Regardless of what you think might be going on, the conversation is pointless. Joss ended it."

"When?"

"A couple days ago."

Grey's eyebrows began to narrow, voice growing hard. "What did you do?"

"How do you know it's something *I* did?"

Grey arched an eyebrow.

Maddox scoffed, retuning to stare out the window. “Who’s at fault is beside the point. It’s done. Over.”

“Of course, who is at fault matters,” Grey said, “because if it were your fault—which I’m sure it was—then you can fix it.”

A bird soared by the window, and Maddox watched it fly high in the sky. “I can’t fix it. She realized I can’t be the man she needs.”

“She said that?” Grey asked, his voice incredulous.

Maddox glanced over his shoulder, finding Grey’s expression incredulous too. “Not in so many words.”

Grey frowned, his eyes narrowed, thoughtful, before he said, “Listen, I saw her that night at the bar when I told her you’d left. She’s a good girl who’s listening to you because you told her not to care about you. But she does. That can’t be faked.”

Maddox turned back to the window and shoved his hands into his pockets, staring out at the trees waving in the wind. “Her caring about me isn’t the issue.” He knew she cared. She’d told him as much. This wasn’t so much about her, as it was about him. “I know there’s something between us.”

“Then what’s the problem?”

Maddox sighed, not sure how to answer Grey. The words seemed too complicated to even explain. His life as he’d known it had shifted, taking a new direction. He lived by logic. He’d made choices for his life because of his past. Relationships were trouble…that was what he knew. Women were difficult…that was what he’d seen. Those were the things he had known and experienced in his life. He had made rules: Don’t date. Don’t love.

That was the way he lived.

Now… "Nothing looks the same, Grey," he admitted, not only to his friend but also to himself. "Nothing feels the same." He paused. Then, still staring out the window, he added, "It's all fucking different now."

"You say that like it's a bad thing."

"She's making me want things I've never wanted before. Christ, I fucking miss her. I don't know what I'm doing without her. How is that not a bad thing?"

A pause. Then, "Man up, you fucking baby."

Maddox glanced over his shoulder. "Excuse me?"

"You heard me," Grey said, slowly rising from his seat, expression tight. "First, you whine about how you shouldn't have touched her. Then, you're lucky enough to get to be with that beautiful, sweet woman, not once, but a handful of times, and you're still fucking whining."

"Grey," Maddox warned.

He stepped forward, eyes narrowed into slits. "You've got this great girl who's cool as shit. She's not clingy. She's perfectly happy accepting the dipshit that you are. And instead of going and loving the hell out of her, you're sitting here with me, whining about missing her. Want me to get you some diapers or a bottle, maybe a blankie so I can tuck you in for naptime?"

Maddox's glare deepened. "Please, Grey, tell me what you really think."

Grey stepped closer, nearly nose-to-nose with Maddox, and did exactly that. "You've learned that your mother, who you thought had abandoned you, didn't. You can't fall on that crutch anymore to avoid getting close to this girl, who, from the way I see it, is the greatest thing that's ever happened to you."

It seemed so simple from Grey's point of view, but… "Our jobs—"

"Are a fucking issue that you can fix," Grey retorted harshly. "You made the mess, yes. Now, go clean it up." He slapped a hand on Maddox's shoulder. "Take my advice, buddy. Go swallow your goddamn pride, do what you need to do to right this situation, and go claim what's fucking yours."

Chapter 13

Day three without Maddox…well, sucked. All through the passing days, Joss thought over her decision, doubted herself, then decided it was for the best. Self-preservation was her only recourse, but it didn't mean she had to like it. Even Emilia had warned her. *Don't fall in love with him.*

Since she'd started back up with Maddox, she'd kept worrying about falling in love with him. The truth was, she'd been in love with him all along. Sure, at first, she was in love with the way he touched her. But then she'd realized the guy behind the sizzling touches was even better. Honorable, sweet at the right moments, strong when he needed to be. For the first time, she couldn't hide behind the shield she kept up to protect herself. He'd been the guy she'd always been looking for, and that's why no one measured up to him.

But he'd recently changed the game. He'd gotten jealous, and that had only made things more confusing. Sure, it would have been easy to hope that he'd be the guy she wanted him to be. Of course, she could hope that he would decide that she was the one for him and they could be together, no longer hiding and pretending they didn't have something special between them. But then she'd end up being like every girl from his past, just like he'd said: *"Girls who think they can change me."*

Hell-to-the-no, she would not be that girl, she decided…*again*… as she held onto the paper cup of her piping-hot coffee and strode through police headquarters, studying how different HQ was than the other precincts in Seattle. Criminals didn't get processed at this downtown location, so for the most part, the building looked cleaner, friendlier. Hell, even fancier.

Once she'd reached the big corner office, she found the man she needed to talk to today sitting behind his desk, reading documents set out before him. The city skyline was a stunning view out the wall of windows behind him as she knocked on the door.

The Chief of Police glanced up and then greeted her with a warm smile. "Joss. What a terrific surprise. Please, come in." He rose immediately and moved to her as she entered his office, then he took her into a warm embrace.

She rested her cheek against his shoulder, hugging him right back. She figured that most rookies found Eric to be a little intimidating, but she never had. Beneath his tough exterior was a big, cuddly bear, whom she had many fond memories of from when she was a child. Most of her summers while growing up had been spent at Eric's family lake house. His daughter, Lana, had been Joss's childhood friend from as early as she could remember until tenth grade. Eric's bitter divorce, and Lana's mother's move to Chicago, was the only reason Lana and Joss weren't still close. Of course, they had tried to keep in touch over email, but sadly, life often got in the way.

When Eric finally leaned away, he gave her a long look. "You're looking well." He tapped her arms and smiled. "And strong. Look what the academy's done to you."

"Toughened me up, for sure." She smiled back.

"Please, take a seat." He waved to the chairs in front of his desk. "How are things?"

There were a million ways to answer that question. Instead of making this conversation too complicated, she took her seat and said, "Things are great. And you?"

"Busy, as always," Eric said, returning to his chair behind his desk. "But it's a good busy. Are they treating you well in the west?"

"Very well, thank you."

Eric leaned forward in his seat and steepled his fingers beneath his chin. "I'm pleased to hear that. And while I love to see you, I'm guessing your visit today isn't personal?"

"Actually, it kinda is." It had taken all her courage to come here today because this could backfire in her face in the most epic of ways, but she'd never let something that scared her before hinder her, so… "I was wondering if it were possible for me to request a transfer?"

Eric's brows drew together, obvious irritation rising to his face. "Did you not tell me the west was treating you well?"

"Oh, they are," she retorted quickly, twining her hands in her lap, desperate to stop the slight shake. "It's not the precinct, or any of my superiors, or fellow cops for that matter. It's personal."

Eric exhaled deeply and leaned back in his chair, watching her carefully. "Did they discover we have a close relationship? I know sometimes the men can be a bit—"

"No." She shook her head. "It's not that."

"Then what exactly is the problem?"

"Well..." She lifted her paper cup in her hand and took a quick sip of her coffee, pausing the conversation, trying to think up a good excuse. She didn't want to out Maddox to Eric, fearing he'd be reprimanded. "I've become involved with someone there, and while it's not affecting my performance now, I fear that it might in the future."

"You've gotten involved, hmm?" Eric remarked with a slow building smile. "How about we don't beat around the bush and say it for what it is—you've been secretly dating Maddox Hunt."

Joss nearly spit her coffee out of her mouth and began coughing.

"Please don't die in my office," Eric mused. "Your father would never forgive me."

"You knew about us?" She wiped her mouth and barely managed, "Why haven't you reprimanded me and suspended him?"

"First, you both have been very discreet. I haven't heard a single whisper about the two of you dating," Eric replied. "Secondly, while the department frowns upon these types of things, unless I have to intervene, I don't. No one can control who they fall in love with."

She blinked, shaking her head to clear the confusion in it. "Okay, wait, hold on, I need a minute. This isn't what I expected to happen here." Eric chuckled, and she blinked, processing. Then she asked, "How do you know I've been seeing him?"

"Before I answer that, since your father would want me to tell you this, let me remind you that you need to be careful with these types of things," he said sternly from behind his desk, being the imposing man he was. "News of affairs like this has a way of getting around stations like wildfire. You don't want something like this hanging over you. I've seen it before. Every promotion is tainted. Every award polluted."

"Yes, sir, I know," she agreed, well aware of those concerns from the very beginning. "Hence the reason I'm here. But please tell me how you knew we were seeing each other."

"Maddox told me."

She sensed the color draining from her face as the world tumbled around her. The telephone on Eric's desk rang, and he held up an index finger then answered the phone. "Yes. Yes. All right. Please hold any other calls. Thank you, Beth." He hung up the phone and explained, "Maddox came to see me at home last night, but to be honest, I had already suspected something might be on going between you two."

"Why?"

Eric picked up a pen, tapping the tip against his desk. "I saw you two in an intimate conversation outside the pub at the retirement party."

Her cheeks warmed, waiting for him to add, *and I saw Maddox kiss you.* When those words never came, she managed, "Why are you being so…okay with all of this?" she wondered her thoughts aloud.

Eric leaned back in his seat, his chair squeaking beneath him before he addressed her again. "Because some rules, Joss, don't even make sense to those who must enforce them."

She blinked again. "Well, I guess, thank you for that."

"You're family. I would have done the same for Lana if she'd been in a similar situation." He hesitated then, and with his head cocked, he added, "But tell me, have things gone south with you and Hunt, is that what this is all about?"

"Not south, just ended," she explained as best she could.

Eric's lips thinned. "Was he respectful?"

"Yes, very," Joss said with a chuckle, not minding Eric's protective side. She didn't see anything wrong with having some good guys looking out for her. "I've got nothing bad to say, so you don't have to worry about it."

Eric regarded her for a long moment, continuing to tap the pen against his desk. "I'm glad to hear that since last night I offered Hunt the position of captain in the east and he accepted the promotion. He'll be moving to the east by the end of the week."

Her stomach roiled, and all the things she thought she knew and thought she'd figured out didn't matter anymore. If that were true, and the work issue between them no longer remained, he obviously didn't feel as attached as she did.

She guessed she should have known that. Even if she was mad at herself for feeling this little moment of pity when she hoped he might have felt the same way she did. Emotions were funny things that sometimes she wished she could tell to *fuck off.* "Did he take the promotion because of our relationship?" she asked.

Eric nodded. "Maddox had originally asked for a transfer, but earlier yesterday, the captain in the east stepped down. We both feel it's also in your best interests for him to transfer out of the west. Did I make the wrong decision by allowing this promotion to happen?"

She let the pain roll through her once more before she stuffed it back into that place where all women stuff their heartache. "No, it's the right decision, and he deserves to be captain."

Everything was as it should be, at least from the outside. She was strong, taking control of her life, not letting a man lead her way. She fought for what she wanted, never accepting less than she deserved.

Even so, it didn't mean she had to like it.

Being the woman she thought she wanted to be somehow felt all wrong without Maddox.

~

LATER THAT NIGHT, Joss entered the Frisky Frikin' with Emilia and Troy, right as the kickoff began on the television screens hung on the wood-paneled walls. She was ready to drink her sorrows away. Sometimes, that was all a woman could do after life disappointed her. Perhaps it was a bad time to realize how much she wanted Maddox in her life. Maybe, deep down, she had hoped that when she walked away, he would wake the hell up and change his mind about relationships. That had never happened. Not even after he transferred to a new station where the conflict lessened. Not even after Eric had so clearly given his approval of them being together. Love sucked. Relationships sucked. Men sucked. She began to regret coming to the pub.

Tonight, as they strode past the bar toward the tables, she found the pub full of cops that she'd met through her father either randomly or at some of the events the police put on in the community. There were a few cops from the west, too. Trying her best not to mope, she followed behind Emilia and Troy as they moved to an empty table. The ruckus from the crowd after the touchdown was a welcome blessing. She couldn't get too lost in her dark thoughts.

Even though Maddox said drinking wasn't a good idea, and she agreed with him, she knew she wasn't drinking because of the death a few days ago. She drank because she had fallen for a guy with huge commitment issues when she'd promised herself that wouldn't happen. Again, love sucked. Relationships sucked. Men sucked.

Troy stopped at one of the round tables and dropped down onto the first stool, followed by Emilia. Joss slid onto her stool across from them—a perfect third wheel. Depressing as shit, but she swallowed the discomfort and knew in half an hour she'd forget all about it with the help of vodka.

Emilia picked up the wine list. Joss stared at them, wondering how they did it, and how they made love look so damn easy. Before she could think better of it, she said, "You guys are so lucky, do you know that? I mean, for cripe's sake, you've been together since high school, and have somehow made it work."

Troy's brows rose before he quickly looked away toward the TV screens, obviously the only amount of girl talk he intended to do tonight.

"Okay, that kinda came out of nowhere." Emilia laughed, placing the wine list back on the table. "Things weren't always so easy, you know. I think every couple has some complications along the way. Don't you think, Troy?"

He gave a pinched expression and nodded, glancing back to the television screens.

Emilia rolled her eyes at her husband before saying to Joss, "Honestly, I don't think there's a magic answer here for why we've worked out. I know people believe in soul mates and all that jazz, and while I think there's some truth to finding the person that makes your soul light up, relationships are all about putting in the hard work. You both have to choose to be in it one hundred percent and then the rest kinda falls into place."

"Exactly," Joss agreed, placing her chin on her hand, trying very hard not to pout. "But what if the other half of the equation doesn't want to?"

"I don't see the waitress anywhere. I'll go grab us drinks." Troy rose and hurried off.

Joss snorted a laugh. "I think we scared him off."

"Please. Any kind of in-depth conversation scares him off." Emilia glanced at her hubby walking toward the bar before adding to Joss, "But that's okay, because that emotionally unavailable teddy bear is all mine." She drew in a big, deep breath before she spoke again, giving Joss a measured look. "Okay, so listen, I know I said falling in love with Maddox would be the worst thing ever, but I'm going to take that back."

Joss's brows rose. "Huh?"

"Oh, don't look so shocked." Emilia grinned. "I've been watching him, even though he doesn't know it. I am the best friend, after all." She gave a big smile, causing her eyes to twinkle. "And let me tell you, girl, he seems different with you."

"I know he cares for me, Emilia," Joss said with a sigh, waving at a couple of cops that her father knew before glancing back at Emilia. "But he can't seem to say it aloud. When I ended things, I gave him the chance to finally acknowledge that we're"—she made quotations with her fingers—"*together*, and he didn't take it."

"Maybe he needs a little time," Emilia offered.

"Maybe what he needs is a big smack to the head." Joss smiled, and Emilia laughed, glancing over Joss's shoulder, clearly looking for her missing husband. "But honestly," Joss added, garnering Emilia's attention again. "How pathetic would it make me if I stayed, knowing that I'd always be his secret, never his girlfriend?"

"Okay, I see your point." Emilia's eyes narrowed with her long sigh before she slapped her hands against the table. "Well, let's hope the idiot wakes the fuck up and sees that you're great for him."

"The idiot has woken the fuck up."

Emilia's eyes widened, and she slapped her hand over her mouth. "I'm so sorry, sir," she said beneath her hand.

Joss froze in her seat, her heart beating a mile a minute. Maddox stood right behind her. Sure, she'd heard his voice, but she could feel the heat of him slowly brushing across her back, sliding down her neck, raising goose bumps all over her flesh.

Emilia slowly lowered her hand. "I…I…shit…I have no idea what to say here." She slapped her hand across her mouth again, eyes huge. "And I just swore," she mumbled.

"I think you've said enough," Maddox said, voice amused. "Besides, I'll forgive you since those words are well deserved." Then his voice shifted, becoming lower, harder. "Joss, look at me."

The air rushed from her lungs as she slowly spun on her stool, and all those things she'd been saying to Emilia didn't matter anymore. Logic couldn't compare to what she felt with Maddox because it wasn't a logic thing. It was emotional. And it was magical, from day one until now. "Is it a coincidence that you're here?" She had to know.

He shook his head.

"You came here to see me?"

He nodded, eyes intent on her, flaring hot with emotion.

"How did you know I'd be here?" she asked, locked in all that powerful energy he was tossing her way.

"I overheard Emilia telling someone at work that you were all coming here tonight."

Joss glanced at Emilia, and her best friend nodded. "I might have said something." She turned to Maddox. "I didn't even see you there."

"He seems to have that spy technique mastered." Joss smiled at Maddox.

His eyes crinkled, but he wasn't moving toward her, just standing near the other table. "I heard that you went and saw my father."

She flinched and recoiled—sure he wouldn't have found that out. "Sorry, I know I probably shouldn't have done that, but I…." She stopped short, beginning to wonder how he'd found out she was there. "Wait, did a nurse tell you? I asked them not to bother you with it."

The pub faded around her as he took a step forward. "My father told me."

"He remembered me?" She gasped.

Maddox grinned. "He did, and do you honestly believe I'd be upset that you went and gave my father a care package?"

She nodded, barely able to breathe, realizing this was how Maddox looked when all his shields were down. Oh, hell, he looked different, the energy between them *felt* different. The hairs on her body rose like static electricity between them.

Still, he stood so far away as he said, "Sugar, you're far sweeter than I think you even realize. Of course, I'm not upset you went there, and of course my father found you unforgettable." His head tilted then, watching her very carefully. "You won't let me stop thinking about you, will you? Every time I try to stay away, you do something that draws me right back."

"Um…" She nibbled her lip, glancing at Emilia, whose mouth was nearly hitting the table, before looking at Maddox again. "I didn't do that to get your attention or anything."

He didn't respond to that but took another step forward, saying instead, "You won't stop being this woman who does everything and anything to put herself into the spots in my soul no one could ever reach."

She could barely catch her breath, her heart now in her throat. "I'm not doing that on purpose."

That left brow of his lifted. "And yet you do it every single time, don't you? Again and again, somehow you make me forget every rule and make me want things I've never wanted before."

After a quick look around the pub, she noted that they were drawing a crowd. Too many eyes were on them, including Sandy's, a well-known gossiper in the west. Joss frowned, turning to Maddox, and whispering, "Maybe we shouldn't talk about this here."

"There's nowhere else I'd rather be," he retorted, freezing her in her seat. His soft, gentle expression said so much without saying anything at all. Something had changed in him. Something big. "I found out yesterday that my mother died a week after she left us. That's why she never came back. My father never told me because he was too ashamed. Even if I understand his reasons, I can't live in the same shadow I've been living in. And do you know why?"

"Why?" she heard herself whisper, feeling slightly detached.

"I refuse to do what he did and make the same mistakes he made." Maddox took another step toward her. "I want to be the man you need me to be to make you happy, not a man who disappoints you."

The world faded around her. Only him, that's all she saw. "I don't want to change you."

A slow smile spread across his face. "And that, sugar, is what makes you, *you,* but when it comes to this, it's not up to you." His voice deepened a little as his gaze roamed over her face, like he was searching for answers and had somehow found them. "I kept wondering what it was about you that made you unforgettable from that first night I touched you."

She blinked, glancing from side-to-side. He was admitting things very publicly. Sure, she knew both their jobs were no longer at risk, but still, Maddox had to know that the cops would gossip about this. "Um, Maddox, what are you—"

He took another step toward her, the heat of his body closing in on her, stealing her voice, as he asked, "You know what I realized?"

"What?" she barely managed.

"I'm in love with you." Her mouth dropped open, and he laughed softly at the shock in her expression. "Yeah, I know, it surprised me, too. But that's what made you so different. You got right into here"—he pointed to his chest—"so easily, I didn't even see it happening. And once you were there, there was no letting you go." He paused, shutting his eyes for a moment, and when they reopened, heady emotion filled their depths. "I won't walk away from the woman I love, and I promise I won't hurt you for loving me back."

He lifted his hand, cupping her face, and while she leaned into his touch, tears filled her eyes. "So, Joss, I have one last question to ask you. Will you date me?"

She smiled through the tears, sliding a little more off her stool, getting closer to him. "Date a heartbreaker, would that be wise?"

"Probably not, it's very risky," he replied with a grin.

She angled her head and stared into his eyes and saw her future. Not a dull moment, she was sure. Love was messy and crazy and wild, and she knew behind it all, she wanted to experience it with the one guy who made it an adventure. Somehow, he didn't want to change her. She didn't want to change him. And yet, they had changed enough to be perfectly imperfect together. "Yes, Maddox, since I'm completely in love with you, too, I guess it would be all right for us to date."

A smile so big and warm crossed his face before she was in his arms. The crowd in the pub roared, whistled, and clapped, and he kissed her exactly like the first time her lips had met his.

That one time in a nightclub that had changed her life forever.

Chapter 14

After Joss had gotten through the awkwardness of everyone clapping at them on their way out the pub's door, she followed Maddox to his house. She had apologized profusely to Emilia for bailing on their drinks, but of course, Emilia understood. In fact, she'd pushed Joss toward the door after a hug of a lifetime. There were a thousand things to think of. One being how she was going to tell her parents that she'd gone from single to dating the captain of the east precinct overnight. Her dad would definitely hear about that from his cronies. But she realized as Maddox shut the door behind her and turned to her with a smile that she didn't have to do this alone, and her parents were going to love him.

She wondered what they would do next? They were entering new territory here, and she was curious if things would change a little between them, but his sexy smile told her things hadn't changed all that much.

That left eyebrow arched. "Are you ready to play, sugar?"

"Always, sir." She grinned.

"Wait here for a minute," he said, leaning forward and kissing her on the forehead.

"What are you up to?" she asked.

His grin turned wicked, and instead of answering her, he said, "Take those clothes off while I'm gone. Bra and panties only."

As she watched him move up the stairs as if he had all the time in the world, she set to undressing, leaving her jeans and blouse at the door, remaining in only a white bra and white cotton boyshorts. Hell, given how she'd felt the past few days, she was only too glad she wasn't wearing granny panties.

Only a handful of minutes later, Maddox appeared on the top landing, shirtless, his pants unbuttoned. Heat flooded her, and when he reached her, she said, "I'm one lucky lady."

His mouth twitched. "Believe me, I'm the lucky one here. I'm still counting my blessings that you said yes to date me. But since you've agreed to be mine now, let me have a look at you." He lifted his finger and motioned for her to turn in a circle. She obliged him and turned toward the door, and he groaned, low and deep. He squeezed her right butt cheek, then her left. "Your ass looks incredible in these."

"I thought you only liked fancy, lacy things," she said, spinning back to him.

"On you?" That eyebrow arched. "I like anything, sugar, and sometimes even better…nothing at all."

She swallowed the added moisture in her mouth at the way he looked at her—like she was truly *his*—before he pulled a blindfold from his back pocket. Darkness soon slid over her eyes as the covering settled into place. She shivered when he stepped in behind her, sliding his fingers down her spine before he kissed her shoulder.

"I'm going to hide," he murmured. "You're going to find me. Then I'll reward you."

She exhaled as the strength and heat at her back vanished when he stepped away. Her eyes were shut beneath the blindfold, but she noticed that she could hear him stride forward. She smiled and listened carefully to his footsteps. Within seconds, it became instantly obvious that he'd gone upstairs.

Thump…thump…thump…

She counted each step, and by the tenth, she knew he hadn't gone into the bedroom. The footsteps came overhead, telling her that he'd traveled farther down the hallway.

Then *silence.*

Silence that told her the chase was on. A chase not necessarily easy half-nude. Slowly, barefoot, she made her way up the stairs, holding onto the railing. Once at the top, she counted the steps that she'd heard him make. The silence around her was thick and heavy. All she could hear were her harsh breaths and her heart hammering in her ears.

Soon, she'd find him. Her pussy drenched with anticipation.

She held her hands out in front of her, ensuring she didn't bump into anything until suddenly those hands touched smooth, warm, and hard skin. "Caught you," she said with a smile.

"Good girl," he murmured, sliding his hands around to her ass, squeezing her cheeks. "Now for that reward, sweetheart." He took her hand, leading her somewhere that took her another seven steps to get there.

Again, the strength of his warm body came at her back when he gathered up her hair, placing it over her shoulder. His hands stroked her body from her face to her neck to the curve of her side to her bottom, there wasn't a single part of her untouched by him. She moaned when his fingers tickled her inner thighs, traveling higher until he slipped his fingers inside her boyshorts and stroked her soaking-wet sex.

"You like finding me, hmmm?" he observed.

She moaned, dropping her head back on his shoulder. "Now that I have you, I never want to lose you."

"You never will." He lowered his lips to her neck, his finger gone from inside her boyshorts. She shivered as his hands traveled over her while he returned to her front. He unhooked her bra, sliding it off her shoulders, then he reached down and removed her boyshorts. His mouth was on hers a moment later, and that's all she knew…all she cared about as she melted into the promise of pleasure.

When he backed away, the cold void of his departure sank in deep, and she whimpered for his return. Yet again, she stood there in the darkness, waiting for whatever he planned to do next. Which came only a second later when something soft dragged against her arm.

She sighed and softened as he began wrapping the rope around her upper body. First, the soft strands slid across the back of her neck, and then she began to feel the tugs against her torso as he placed knots along her front.

His fingers paused when he kissed her shoulder, saying softly, "Grab your forearms behind your back." She did as told, and he kissed her neck, "That's my girl." He stepped in behind her and began sliding the rope through her arms until they were bound tightly at her back. "Beautiful," he murmured, sliding his fingers along the curve of her breast.

Again, he moved away.

She tilted her head, hearing a *click,* then she understood why, as he returned to her and slid a wet silicone object across her slit.

"Spread your legs," he said, causing her to shiver.

She slid her feet apart, letting him insert the dildo inside her, obviously coated in lube from the container he'd opened. The dildo wasn't small in nature, by any means, but not as big as Maddox either. He gently pushed the toy up inside her until she felt a flatter piece of silicone press across her clit. The tease of being full and the pressure was enough to make her circle her hips, eager for more.

"Ah, you like this?"

"Yes, sir."

His low chuckle brushed across her, while he began to fasten straps around her hips and legs until the dildo rested inside her and the vibe pressed tightly against her clit. "I'm sure you'll like this more," he said, then the vibe against her clit came to life—a slow, weak buzz tickling her sensitive bud.

Again, he moved away, like before, but now, the pause was longer. So long that she assumed he watched her while the vibrator teased her and the dildo stretched her. Time passed slowly, and only when she began to breathe deeper and moan a little louder did he return to her. Not to her front, this time he moved behind her, spreading her butt cheeks.

She gasped as sudden wetness spread across her anus and there was pressure pushed against her puckered knot. She knew she could say *red* and stop this, but she didn't want to, trusting him. The pressure gave her more, and more was what she wanted.

Her eyes rolled into the back of her head when he kissed her spine, slowly swirling his tongue across her flesh. "Push out a little, sugar."

She moaned against the pressure, breathing deeply as the new toy pressed against her anus. He stayed silent, being calm and gentle, while her mind fought to understand the discomfort at her bottom, mixed with the pleasure deep inside. She released a long, slow breath as the toy settled inside her, filling her body in ways she'd never been.

"Perfect," he said, kissing her shoulder.

She wanted to answer him, she did, but at that moment, he chose to remove the blindfold. There were no words. She blinked a couple of times, clearing her eyesight until she realized she stood in his bathroom. And the way he'd positioned her, she was staring at herself, bound in black rope like she wore a black bikini top without the fabric covering her breasts. Her arms were back behind her, with a very naked and erect Maddox next to her.

"See how pretty you are?" He cupped her breast and massaged the one, tweaking her nipple. "How perfect you look?"

Again, she tried to respond, but…*click.*

In the mirror, she watched her eyes widen and cheeks flush deep in color as the vibrator turned to a higher speed.

"Enjoy this," he said with a smile, before kissing her shoulder again and stepping in behind her.

With his smoldering eyes locked on hers in the mirror, he clicked the button again and now the dildo began vibrating, too. Her knees went weak, and she had to lock them, ensuring she didn't fall over. He watched her intently as he clicked the remote again.

"Oh, shit." She dropped her head back against his shoulder as he pinched her nipple tightly. His hand slid up to her neck, holding a little tighter than before as he began grinding his rock-hard cock against her bottom, taking pleasure he wanted from her.

Click.

She gasped against the harsh buzz on her clit, and his low chuckle only made her shiver harder. She was barely able to watch him move to the bathroom counter. There, she watched him apply a condom and then add generous amounts of lube to his cock.

When he returned to her, he grasped her chin. "Do I get to have all of you, Joss?"

"Yes, sir," she barely managed.

He stepped in behind her and slipped his fingers between her butt cheeks, stroking around the butt plug. His low groan told her he liked how she looked, ready and stuffed full, as he slowly withdrew the butt plug, placing it on a towel next to him. Then he stepped in close, held her hip, and looked at her through the mirror. "Ever imagined what it'd be like to be with two men?"

She nodded, gasping and quivering.

A slow smile spread across his face before he buried his face against her neck and licked her from shoulder to ear as he whispered, "I'll never share you, sugar, but I'll do my best to fulfill every one of your fantasies." The tip of his cock pressed against her puckered knot. "Breathe out." Then he pushed his hips forward, pressing past the tight rim. "Now breathe in."

She groaned, her legs trembling, as he slowly inched his way inside her, stretching her in ways she'd never been stretched. His fingers dug into her hip as he took his time, being gentle until he settled in deep, past the tight rim. His eyes shut, pleasure washing over his expression. She exhaled the breath she'd be holding, panting, overwhelmed by him. By it all.

When he opened his eyes, he began shifting his hips, slow and gentle.

She moaned, trying to understand the sensations. The intense pleasure on her clit. The fullness in her pussy. The tightness and pressure in her anus. She gasped and moaned and grunted against it all, until he began shifting easier, her body far more accepting, and he moved a little faster now. His one hand slid over her breast, and he massaged her before his fingers moved toward her nipple where he pinched the bud in his tight grip.

Three things happened all at once in the most unexpected way. The vibe kicked up to the final speed. The fullness she experienced morphed into hot pleasure flooding her. And she wasn't sure if she screamed or bucked or jerked or even if he had climaxed with her, all she knew was she orgasmed…and orgasmed…and orgasmed…until suddenly she wasn't orgasming anymore, she was lying in a heap on the cold bathroom floor.

Minutes passed in blur of confusion. She couldn't remember when he'd withdrawn his cock or removed the vibe and dildo, all she recalled was being wiped down with a warm cloth before he removed the rope then took her in his arms.

Now, being carried from the bathroom into the bedroom, she rested her head against his warm, damp chest. At the bed, he lay her down in the middle, and the mattress dipped when he joined her.

On his side, he ran his fingers down her stomach, staring into her eyes. She lay there, watching him, too. Silent. Recovering. For many, many, long minutes. Only when her mind returned fully did she dare talk. "So, is this the kinda love I have to look forward to?"

He gave her his sexy half-grin. "Yes, and it's the best kind of love there is."

"Oh, yeah, what kind of love do we have?" she asked, snuggling into him, feeling sore in the best kind of way.

He gathered her in his arms, pulling her as close as she could get, and chuckled. "Filthy, dirty love, of course."

"Filthy, dirty love?" She laughed. "Sounds promising."

"Oh, sugar, but it is that."

"And will it always be?"

He stared at her and promised, "Always. Forever."

Epilogue

From inside his kitchen, Maddox glanced out at his backyard through the window above the sink, where things had begun again for him and Joss. Exactly one year after his last party for the new rookies and his fellow cops, the backyard looked different now, or maybe he simply saw the world through new eyes.

He grabbed the plate of burgers off the counter and then exited through the patio door. From her spot at the outdoor sitting area around the fire pit, Joss smiled at him before she focused on her mother again. How beautiful she looked there with her wedding ring sparkling off the string of lights wound around their pergola, lighting up the outdoor space.

So many changes had happened, that nothing quite looked the same anymore. But they were the best kinds of changes. Their whirlwind adventure into dating had only lasted three months before Maddox insisted that she move in with him, and three days after that, he put a ring on her finger. Now, Maddox and Joss had been married for four months, and he liked all the finishing touches she'd put on the house.

Though the changes weren't only personal, they were professional, too. While Maddox was the captain in the east, Joss stayed in the west, where in another two years, she'd likely get the promotion to detective that she'd wished for. The truth was, as much as Maddox feared that his career would overshadow hers, her connection to the cheif kept everyone's lips tightly shut. Besides, in the year that she'd been a cop, her work ethic stood apart from any connection she had to any of her superiors.

The warm air brushed across him as he moved to the grill, finding Grey in an eerily similar spot as where he'd been last year when Joss had come back into Maddox's life and changed everything.

"You know," Grey said when Maddox reached him. "I still think you're the luckiest bastard out there." He motioned to the rookies, who stood off near the bar quietly mingling among themselves. "Every year, I think they actually get hotter."

"And every year, they also get younger," Maddox reminded him, placing the burgers on the hot grill.

Grey frowned, tipping his beer at Maddox. "Careful. You're beginning to sound like my mother."

Maddox barked a laugh. "Then kill me."

"Seriously, though," Grey added with a smile, glancing at Joss, who sat with her parents over on the patio couches. "Look at you two, you've become totally domesticated."

"Even more than you know." Maddox added the burgers to the grill, knowing what he said next would cause a ripple. "Soon there will be three of us."

Grey's head snapped around to Maddox, eyes wide. "She's pregnant?"

Maddox smiled. "Just three months now."

"Congrats, man." Grey yanked Maddox into him, smacking his back in a rough man-hug. "You're going to be a father." He leaned away, giving Maddox another hard smack on the back, grinning from ear-to-ear. "My mother will be so pleased."

"I'm sure she will." Maddox laughed.

Grey looked at Joss again before leaning back against the post, folding his arms. "You know, a year ago I never would've believed this would be where you ended up."

Maddox began flipping the burgers, one by one. "Doesn't it make you wonder where you'll be a year from now?"

Unusual softness filled Grey's eyes. "I'll probably be right back here, holding onto your sweet babe while you're flipping burgers for your new rookies."

"Or you'll be holding onto *your* wife," Maddox offered.

Grey snorted and shook his head. "Nah, buddy, the domesticated shit is for you, not me."

Maddox smiled and glanced down at the burgers cooking on the grill. Once, he'd thought along those same lines, too, and now he knew all it took was one woman to blow that thought into a hundred pieces. He hoped Grey found what he had, but he also wasn't planning to get all gushy and tell Grey that either.

When he'd flipped some of the new patties, he began taking off the cooked ones from earlier and placing them on a serving plate. He kept two off to the side, and called to the crowd, "Burgers up."

"I'd better grab one before they're gone. These people are like vultures," Grey said, rushing forward and making himself a plate.

Maddox laughed to himself and added a couple of buns to the two burgers he'd kept aside and then approached Joss and her parents. She was laughing at something her mother had said, but when she caught sight of him, she smiled as he set one burger on Joss's plate and another on her mother's. "Dinner's up, ladies," he told them.

Joss's father snorted. "Better stop it, Maddox. You're starting to make me look bad."

"Well, sir." Maddox straightened and shoved his hands into his pockets. "You've got quite the head start on impressing your ladies. I need to catch up."

Her father chuckled softly as he rose from his seat. He squeezed Maddox's shoulder in a familiar embrace Maddox had grown to enjoy this past year before heading off to fetch his dinner.

"Oh, I'd better get another drink, too," her mother said, rising from her chair. When Maddox reached for her wineglass, she added, "You don't need to spoil me all the time, Maddox. I've got this."

"Yes, ma'am." He smiled, letting her take the glass from his hand.

Once she'd headed off to fetch her drink, Maddox took her seat, pulling it closer to Joss. "Doing okay, sugar?" he asked, stroking her cheek.

Her nose scrunched, and she frowned at her burger. "I think you'd better take that away from me." Her concerned eyes came to his, mouth pinched tightly.

Swiftly, he grabbed the plate and moved it behind him, not in the direction of the wind. "Burgers are on the list of what you can't eat?"

"Apparently," she said with a sigh, placing a hand on her lower belly. "Honestly, at this rate, our kid is going to be a vegetarian."

"That will never happen," Maddox said seriously with a firm shake of his head, placing his hand on her belly. "My son will like eating meat as much as he enjoys hunting for it."

Joss gave him a sweet smile, placing her hand on top of his. "And how do you know we're having a boy?"

"I don't, of course, but I have a feeling."

"A feeling, hmm?" She stroked her fingers across his hand, looking up at him through her lashes. "But what if it's a girl, will you be disappointed?"

He chuckled softly, rubbing her belly. "Of course, not. That just means I'll need my shotgun for other reasons than hunting."

"You're not going to threaten our child's crushes." Joss frowned at him.

He smiled. "Wanna bet?"

Joss barked a laugh, and he loved that laugh. So happy. So free. So perfect. So his. "You'll never change, will you? Always the broody, alpha guy?"

"No," he said, "And you forgot something on my title, didn't you?"

She hesitated. Then chuckled again. "Sex God."

"That's it, sugar. And you know why I won't change?"

"Why?" She smiled.

He cupped her nape, pulling her close, and before he sealed his mouth across hers, he murmured, "Because you like it."

And he'd make sure she always liked the adventure and loved him. Today. Tomorrow. And Always.

Acknowledgments

Much love to my family; my readers; my editor, Christa; my copy editor, Chelle; my assistant, Michelle; the kick-ass authors in my sprint group; and my cover designer, Sara. This book couldn't have happened without all of you!

By STACEY KENNEDY

FILTHY DIRTY LOVE

Heartbreaker

Skirt Chaser (coming soon)

DIRTY LITTLE SECRETS

Bound Beneath His Pain

Tied to His Betrayal

Restrained Under His Duty (coming soon)

CLUB SIN

Claimed

Bared

Desired

Freed

Tamed

Commanded

Mine

Stay up-to-date with Stacey's new releases by visiting these links:

Stacey's newsletter sign-up:

www.staceykennedy.com/newsletter

Website:

www.staceykennedy.com

Facebook:

https://www.facebook.com/authorstaceykennedy

Instagram:

https://www.instagram.com/kennedy.stacey/

Twitter:

https://twitter.com/Stacey_Kennedy

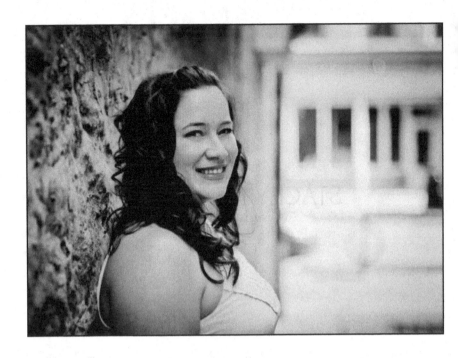

STACEY KENNEDY is the *USA Today* bestselling author of the Dirty Little Secrets and Club Sin series. She writes deeply emotional romances about powerful men and the wild women who tame them. When she's not writing sensual stories, she spends her time in southwestern Ontario with her real life hero, her husband, their two young children, and her other babies: a mini labradoodle named Jax and a chocolate labrador named Murphy. Stacey is a proud chocolate, television show, Urban Barn, and wine addict. She likes her heroes in her books like she likes her coffee…strong and hot!

vstaceykennedy.com
Facebook.com/authorstaceykennedy
@Stacey_Kennedy

Read on for an excerpt
from Stacey Kennedy's Dirty Little Secret series:

BOUND BENEATH HIS PAIN

A Loveswept eBook Original

Published in the United States by Loveswept, an imprint of Random House, a division of Penguin Random House LLC, New York.

ebook ISBN 9781101882566

Cover design: Okay Creations
Cover photograph: © FXQuadro/Shutterstock

randomhousebooks.com

CHAPTER 1

Allie

"Get here. Pronto. Shit is going down!"

There are only three reasons my real estate assistant, Liv Sloan, sent me the vague text on Monday morning.

One, the deal for my last clients, who fled the lively Haight-Ashbury area to raise their family in the quiet and quaint Cole Valley district, fell apart.

Two, our boss is in a mood.

Three, a pair of Liv's beloved high-heel shoes suffered a wretched death.

Stuffed inside the elevator, a block away from Union Square, with rank perfume smells tickling my nose, I wonder over Liv's message. All three reasons are totally up her alley. She's dramatic, but in a cute, funny way that I love.

When the elevator doors chime open, I ease my way out, entering Richardson Real Estate, and frown. While I love my job, the offices are a whole other thing. They're in need of a *major* upgrade, which is the very reason I'm late today. I'd never meet clients in this run-down horror show.

I pass the empty waiting room, scrunching my nose against the stale smell hanging in the air, then pick up my pace, turning the corner down the main hallway, finding Liv standing by the watercooler near our cubicles.

"You're not going to believe what's happened," she says, practically bursting with energy.

"Aliens have invaded Earth?" I offer.

"What?" She gives her head a slight shake, her brown curls bouncing on her shoulders. "Guess again."

"Santa came early and brought you new Louboutin shoes?"

She gives me a playful nudge, her big, round brown eyes squinting. "Ha, I can only wish! Holt has bought out Richardson."

I pause, waiting for her to say she's joking. "You're serious?"

She nods. "Very serious."

A knot of worry tightens in my belly then I force myself to go numb. I'm a top-selling agent at Richardson. My job can't be in jeopardy. This has to be good news, right? Still, I can't wrap my head around it. Holt has made billions of dollars dealing in commercial properties. Richardson's sales are only in the multi-millions, with a handful of agents selling middle-income homes. Sure, that's Richardson's strength in the San Francisco market, but why would Holt want to add it to their portfolio? Isn't the middle-class market messy pocket change to them? "What in the world does Holt want with Richardson?" I voice my thoughts.

Liv gets herself a drink from the watercooler and then faces me. "From what I gathered, Holt wants to gobble up the entire real estate market. Businesses, high-class homes, middle-class homes; they want it all. Including taking the top agents at Richardson into Holt."

Greedy pricks. They can't be satisfied having a corner of the market to make their billions, they need to suck the whole damn thing dry. I lean against the cubicle next to us, my back straight as a pencil. "So, their plan is to swallow Richardson up?"

"To be honest, I don't really know what the plan is." She leans closer to me and tells me quietly, "They offered me a job at Holt. Which I guess means they're taking you, too."

"Indeed, that is the plan," says a strong male voice.

Oh, shit!

I hesitantly glance sideways and unfamiliar sparkling blue eyes hold mine. "I take it you're Allison Parker?" the stranger asks.

"That's right," I reply. "But you can call me *Allie.*"

"It's nice to meet you, Allie." He offers a handshake. "I'm Anderson West, COO at Holt."

I admire his blue suit while shaking his hand, thinking not only does this forty-something-year-old man have some serious style, but the Holt staff is very professional. Our own CEO, Henry, is typically found wearing loose-fitting khakis and sweaters to cover an aging midsection.

Anderson releases my hand and adds, "I take it Liv has filled you in on what you missed at the meeting."

I smile. "Yes. I'm all caught up."

"Excellent, saves me from repeating myself." He shoves one hand into his pant pocket, straightening his spine. "As with Liv, we'd like to offer you a position at Holt." He hands me a sealed white envelope with my name on the front. "Please know that the terms are negotiable. If you want we can discuss—"

"Ah, the straggler has finally decided to grace us with her presence." Another unknown voice booms, from a man who appears to my other side. This one with even a more raspy, gravelly tone.

I gulp, realizing *who* the smooth silky voice must belong to, *Micah Holt.* His bluish-gray eyes narrow on me and my breath is *gone,* as the air whooshes out of the room. Everyone in San Francisco knows the famous billionaire, *the tabloids make sure of that. This hot playboy is a weekly feature, not that I read the rags that often, but you can't miss his face plastered on them as you wait in the grocery store lines.*

Confronted by the real man, I understand why the tabloids are obsessed with him. The power he exudes is magnetizing, raising the hairs on my arms. He owns the space around him, making everyone else disappear. All I know is his sexy-as-hell eyes on me and how that act alone warms me from the inside out. I raise my hand and smile. "Hello, that's me, I'm Allie, the straggler."

By the arch of his brow, I assume the first impression I'm putting forward surprises him. Which it does me too, as I'm not usually a smart-ass, but he's rattling me. I'm drawn to him, no matter that I don't want to be, because I *know* this guy is a bad idea.

And I know that so definitely because I know his type. My half-brother is cut from the same cloth as Micah. I bet he's a man who works from eight in the morning until eleven at night. He's probably a guy who only has relationships to financially or sexually benefit him.

Regardless of what I *know,* the instant attraction is rich with velvety promise.

One side of his mouth slowly arches in the beginning of a smile and he finally murmurs, "Allie."

A shifting feeling happens near my heart, a pang of sorts, leaving me aware of the delicious burn he's stirring inside me. Oh, this guy is smooth. He doesn't say someone's name; instead, he rolls it off his tongue, savoring the syllables. Micah's got game, no question, and I realize I'm going to have to be on my toes around him.

Of course part of my problem is that I haven't dated in over a year and my force field is thinning. Perhaps if I'd listened to Liv and stopped being so damn picky, this guy's well-played tactics wouldn't be affecting me.

Micah's hand moves toward me then, his strong fingers clasp mine, and there's nothing professional about this handshake or my reaction to *him.* My nipples pucker beneath my bra into hard points and heat pools low in my body. Which by the slight grin on his face, I'm sure he's well aware.

Anderson clears his throat, interrupting a moment that seems to have gone on way too long. "As I was saying to Allie, we can discuss the terms of her offer, if she would like."

Smoky eyes on mine, undressing me where I stand, Micah slowly releases my hand. "Let me handle this negotiation." He takes the envelope from Anderson. "Please follow me, Allie."

Obviously I'm not the only one surprised, because the look on Anderson's face tells me this isn't normal behavior, and Liv notices, too, grinning and winking at me. I roll my eyes at her enjoyment at my expense, and exhale loudly, following Micah into the meeting room, noticing now that some of my peers are watching this parade.

Ugh. *Get control of yourself, Allie.* It's a guy in a suit. Well, a totally hot guy in a suit, but still a guy that I met a hundred times growing up. Famous. Spoiled. Rich. Arrogant. Not the guy for me.

I take my seat at the rectangular office table, inhaling the fragrance à la Robertson—the moldy smell is worse in the conference rooms—reminding myself I'm a professional woman. I'm not one to be charmed by a man who thinks he's all that. And I won't let his good looks, charisma, and sexy smile distract me from negotiating my job.

He slowly opens his jacket, exposing his wide shoulders and thick chest beneath his black vest, all to tempt me, I'm sure. What's frustrating is how much it's beginning to work—my nerve endings tingle, and more and more warmth is sliding down between my thighs.

I expect him to begin negotiations, but he asks a question totally out of the blue: "Tell me a bit about yourself."

My belly quivers with the low silky tenor of his voice and the power it has over me. He's not looking at me. He's fucking me with his eyes. Each long linger he gives me is like he's imagining where he'd kiss me. The passion is right there and is so tempting I want to grab the flirtation between us and play with it a while. Boy, do I ever. But I *can't,* I remind myself.

Micah lives a life I don't want. A life of privilege that I once lived myself.

My mind leaves the meeting room, returning to a past that I wish I could forget. Shortly after my fifteenth birthday, my parents lost their lives in a plane crash. Fortunately, my older by ten years and very rich half-brother swooped in to save me from foster care and took me in. But a life of privilege isn't the one I want and it's not the life my mother would've wanted for me either. She wanted me to make my own mark on the world, and that's exactly what I've done. It's the very reason no one at Richardson—even Liv—knew I had millions in a trust fund.

I blink into the present, give Micah my most professional smile, and set to answering his question. "I'm twenty-five. Born in San Francisco. I've been a real estate agent for five years."

His sculpted lips press tight. "I'm sure you know I didn't want you to recite your resume."

"Yes, I'm sure I know that, too." I grin.

Judging by his soft chuckle, he's enjoying the game between us. His playfulness isn't helping the weight in my belly, but I need to keep my wits about me. This guy is so wrong for me that I know better than to give him a single flirtatious smile.

"We're all business, then?" he practically purrs.

"On to negotiations," I confirm.

He finally breaks eye contact to acquaint himself with the terms of my employment offer before addressing me again. "Please don't feel nervous or unsure in what you want during these negotiations. I'm here to listen and discuss what you feel you deserve."

Coming from any other guy, this speech would seem sweet and thoughtful. As it is coming from a guy dressed in an expensive tailored black suit, while he is leaning back in his seat, chest out, chin high, I refrain from snorting. Powerful men are all the same. And I certainly don't need him to hold my hand. "Thank you. That's very kind."

His eyes narrow at my demure tone of voice, then his mouth twitches. Obviously he sees the amusement in this scenario; not to be shallow, but I am Richardson's top producer—I think I can "negotiate" a contract. *Jeez.*

I keep silent; he grabs out a pen from his jacket pocket, never taking his eyes off me. I shiver—not from the coolness of the room, but because of his intensity. He exudes a frightening amount of power. And a confidence that I've rarely seen in a man his age; if I recall correctly, the tabloids pegged him at thirty-five.

The strength he projects seems hauntingly dark. But it's not a darkness I want to run from. It's a darkness that draws me in. A darkness that I almost want to absorb.

I shake the thoughts from my head. Let's be logical here, this guy has nothing to offer me except lust. And I want more than that when it comes to a relationship; I want love, trust, and, dare I say, maybe even the white picket fence? Which I suppose explains why I'm still very single.

He taps his pen against the paper. "Go ahead and negotiate your terms."

I glance at the document before me, thinking of my very successful half-brother and the lessons he taught me about negotiation. *Ask for more than you think you'll get, because then you'll end up somewhere in the middle,* he once told me.

"This is all great, and the health benefits are appreciated," I say to Micah, keeping my eyes on the papers. "However, I have some conditions besides what I'm seeing here."

"Name them," he tells me.

I note the commission on the papers, which is the same as I get at Richardson—the offer states that I'll receive 2.5 percent of the purchase price as my commission from the sales, then out of the money I earn on the deal, I'll give Holt 30 percent as their cut. I've done my competitive research over the years, just to make sure I knew what the market would bear should I ever leave Richardson. "In section four where the commission is noted, I want Holt's commission adjusted from 30 percent to 20 percent of my earnings." I watch Micah's brows shoot up and add, "And if you haven't already given Liv a salary increase, then she'll need that, too."

A slow, dangerous smile crosses his face. "Anything else to adjust?"

I pause, ponder, then shake my head. "No, that's all."

"You drive a hard bargain," he says, considering me.

Of course I did, my big bro taught me all about business. I figured Micah probably operated the same way. I had to address him with the same intensity he shows me or I won't get his respect. "It's not a bargaining technique," I correct him, mirroring his slow, dangerous smile. "It's simply what I deserve based on the market today."

He leans back in his chair, regarding me with a long look. "It seems you have more experience than what I'd originally thought. Where did you work before Richardson?"

"Nowhere."

"No internship out of university?"

"I never went to university. I started at Richardson right out of high school, then obtained my real estate license." Well, first I traveled Europe for a year with my best friend, Taylor Erikson, on a trip of self-discovery. The only discovery we made is that I can drink Taylor under the table. I became a real estate agent after working as a receptionist at Richardson, during which time I studied for and obtained my license. But these all are things he doesn't need to know.

His smoky eyes narrow again. "You have no other business experience?"

"No, I'm afraid not." Dammit, I need to dial back the confidence a tad. Everyone has secrets they hold dear and I have mine, too. My past isn't something I want advertised. "Those are my terms. Are you in agreement?"

He taps his fingers against the table and then begins to swirl them in a slow circle against the dark wood, those eyes directly on my face. I'm ashamed by the way my lower body clenches, as I'm wondering how that touch would feel against my naked skin.

I force myself to look at his face when he finally addresses me again. "Holt will take 25 percent of your commission, not the 20 percent that you're asking for or the 30 percent we originally offered. Will that suffice?"

I pretend to ponder his offer—25 percent is incredible. "Yes, I'll agree to that."

He clasps his hands on the table, and I feel like he's stripping me layer by layer. It's intrusive, but I'm not opposed to it. More heat spreads through me, tempting me to move a little closer to him.

I order myself to stay put when he arches a single brow. "You do realize that you'll have to deliver high sales to prove you're worth what you're asking for."

I nod. "Of course." And I would prove my worth. Or Liv and I would, I should say.

A long moment of silence settles between us. He's still regarding me, and within his confident stare I feel like he's hiding something, or at least that's how it seems. I don't know exactly what it is, but it's intriguing nonetheless.

His jaw clenches twice before he speaks again. "Well then, let's hope you can deliver on the promises you are making here." He moves his pen quickly over the document, changing the terms, and initialing the changes. "You'll need to bring three signed copies of the offer when you arrive at Holt tomorrow morning."

"Perfect." I accept the papers from him. "Now, one more thing before we finalize this."

Both of his brows shoot up. I can only guess he's not used to having anyone dismiss a meeting—which, of course, is exactly why I said it. But the other reason is I'm concerned about my employer. "Before I sign this contract and agree to move to Holt, what is going to happen to Richardson?"

By the way he straightens in his seat, I wonder if I hit a nerve. I realize I'm asking a question that is totally none of my business, and when he folds his arms, closing himself off to me, I become a little nervous about his answer.

"You're worried about a company you're considering leaving?"

I can't get a read on him. His expression is showing very little, so I reply, "Richardson gave me my start. The way I see it, I owe it some loyalty. And I want to know what your plans are."

He's watching me closely; a section of his jet-black stylish hair falls free. "Why does it matter? Richardson's clients will be moved to Holt and all deserving employees will be hired on in some capacity."

"Exactly my point," I fire back. "What makes them deserving? Is your decision based on how much they made last year?"

Finally there's a crack in his unreadable expression, and I can tell by the widening of his eyes that my question surprises him. "What they bring into the company is taken into consideration." He pauses, and his attention lingers a little too long on me, like he's sizing me up. "Would you expect it not to be?"

"In business, I *do* expect that," I say with a shrug. "But what if they had a bad year? Take Sandy, she's a longtime agent for Richardson—she lost her husband this past year and has been struggling." His lips part, but I continue before he can cut me off. "Another employee, Jacob, recently found out that his young daughter has cancer. These are things that you don't know about the people who work here. So, yes, I'm asking what will happen to them."

He scrapes his fingers across his square jaw, and I notice his face is ridiculously chiseled, like the rest of him. "Your concern here is that your friends—"

"They're not my friends," I correct him.

He snorts softly. "You're *this* worried about co-workers?"

"Yes." Because if I didn't say this now no one would. Micah *is* intimidating. I'm experienced at handling men like Micah and ensuring they don't railroad people. These are things that need to be said, because Sandy and Jacob both deserve to keep their jobs, regardless that they had low sales last year.

Money isn't everything.

His finger continues to stroke his chin from left to right when he asks, "If I say I plan on dismantling Richardson and can't save every job, you would refuse to move to Holt, even if that means you would lose your job?"

"Yes."

"Why?"

I can tell he's honestly interested, not judging me, so I'm bluntly honest with him. "I refuse to work for a company that can't see past the bottom line and doesn't care for its employees and treat them as people."

He's watching me again, and yet he's completely unreadable. He wants inside my head, I'm sure of it, and I feel, for this second, that if I let him in he'll awaken me in ways I've never known. I'm tempted to reach across the table and—

A knock on the door jerks my focus there, finding Anderson peeking his head inside the meeting room. "Yes?" he drawls.

I'm reeling, fighting my way back from the promise of satisfaction in Micah's eyes, and trying to understand how in the hell he alerted Anderson that he needed him, when Micah rises from his chair. "Instruct the team to stop dismantling the company. Tell them to give me a report on Richardson's financials ASAP. And keep all Richardson staff on board here, unless anyone willingly wants to move to Holt."

Anderson frowns, stepping farther into the office. "Didn't you say shut down this—"

"You heard me." Eyes still intent on me, with that sexy little arch curving the side of his mouth, Micah asks me, "I'll see you at Holt tomorrow, Allie?"

"You will," is all I can say.

And just like that, he's gone, and I'm alone, dragging in heavy breaths through my mouth.

The tabloid headlines at the grocery store spoke of Micah as being ruthless. But that's not the guy I met today. Charming and seductive seems like an impenetrable armor to mask a certain dark intensity about him.

I press my hands flat on the table, hoping the coolness of the wood eases the fire in my veins. My nerve endings are tingling. My panties are soaking wet. But there's a truth I cannot ignore besides the heat he awakens inside of me.

Men like Micah don't do something out of the goodness of their heart. He made this choice because *I* asked him to.

This is his leverage over me.

And now I owe him.

Printed in the United States
by Baker & Taylor Publisher Services